Cast of Characters

Kate Rebel: Matriarch of the Rebel family.

Falcon: The oldest son—the strong one. Reunited with his wife, Leah, and proud father of Eden and John.

Egan: The loner. Married to Rachel Hollister, daughter of the man who put him in jail.

Quincy: The peacemaker. In love with Jenny Walker, his brother's girlfriend.

Elias: The fighter. Falls in love with the archenemy of the family's daughter.

Paxton: The lover. Never met a woman he couldn't have, but the woman he wants doesn't want him.

Jude: The serious, responsible one. Raising his small son alone.

Phoenix: The wild one and the youngest. He's wild and free until Child Protective Services says he's the father of a small boy.

Abraham (Abe) Rebel: Paternal grandfather.

Jericho Johnson: Egan's friend from prison.

Texas Rebels: Quincy

LINDA WARREN

First published in Great Britain 2016
by Mills & Boon, an imprint of Harlequin (UK) Limited,
Large Print edition 2016
Eton House, 18-24 Paradise Road,
Richmond, Surrey, TW9 1SR

© 2015 Linda Warren

ISBN: 978-0-263-06600-5

Printed and bound in Great Britain
by CPI Antony Rowe, Chippenham, Wiltshire

Two-time RITA® Award-nominated and award-winning author **Linda Warren** loves her job, writing happily-ever-after books for Harlequin. Drawing upon her years of growing up on a farm/ranch in Texas, she writes about sexy heroes, feisty heroines and broken families with an emotional punch, all set against the backdrop of Texas. Her favourite pastime is sitting on her patio with her husband watching the wildlife, especially the injured ones that are coming in pairs these days: two Canada geese with broken wings, two does with broken legs and a bobcat ready to pounce on anything tasty. Learn more about Linda and her books at her website, lindawarren.net, or on Facebook, LindaWarrenAuthor, or follow @Texauthor on Twitter.

I dedicate this book to Jaci Siegert,
my goddaughter.
May you always love to read.

Acknowledgements

A special thanks to Linda Stewart, LVN,
for taking time to share her knowledge
and answering my many questions
about nurses and injuries.

And thanks to the
American Paint Horse Association
for sharing their information.

Also, thanks to
Texas A&M Veterinary Clinic
for answering my vet questions.

All errors are strictly mine.

Prologue

My name is Kate Rebel. I married John Rebel when I was eighteen years old and bore him seven sons. We worked the family ranch, which John later inherited. We put everything we had into buying more land so our sons would have a legacy. We didn't have much, but we had love.

The McCray Ranch borders Rebel Ranch on the east, and the McCrays have been a source of stress for my family. They've cut our fences, dammed up creeks to limit our water supply and shot one of our prized bulls. Ezra McCray threatened to shoot our sons if he caught them jumping his fences again. We tried to keep our boys away, but they are boys, young and wild.

One day John was out working and two of our youngest, Jude and Phoenix, were riding together bareback. When John heard shots, he immediately rode to find his boys. They lay on the ground, blood oozing from their heads. Ezra McCray was astride a horse twenty yards away with a rifle in his hand. John drew his rifle and fired, killing Ezra instantly. Both boys survived with only minor wounds. Since my husband was protecting his children, he never spent one night in jail. This escalated the feud that still goes on today.

The man I knew as my husband died that day. He couldn't live with what he'd done and started to drink heavily. I had to take over the ranch and the raising of our boys. John died ten years later. We've all been affected by the tragedy, especially my sons.

They are grown men now and deal with the

pain of losing their father in different ways. One day I pray my boys will be able to put this behind them and live healthy normal lives with women who will love them the way I loved their father.

Chapter One

Quincy: the second son—the peacemaker

The cowboy who couldn't ride away…

Always being the nice guy must have finally brought out the bad boy in Quincy Rebel. There was no other way to explain how he could have fallen in love with Jenny Rose Walker, his brother's girlfriend.

It broke the brothers' code, as told to the Rebel boys by their father: *never betray your brother with a woman. There will be many women in your lives, but a brother will be a brother forever.* Strong words. Their father's words. As the peacemaker in the family, Quincy would not do anything to cause a rift with his brothers or to dishonor his father's memory. This was his heartache. His pain. His secret.

Riding into the barn on his paint stud Red Hawk, he felt sure he could continue to hide his feelings. He dismounted and ran a hand around the back of his neck to unstick his sweaty collar from his skin. The sultry August heat had lingered into the first week of September. Before he'd left at the start of the day, he'd opened both double doors of the barn, and a gentle breeze stirred the heat like a slow-moving fan. The scents of dust and alfalfa filled his lungs.

Quincy bred paint horses and had his own barn and corrals away from the main ranch. He'd picked out the spot near the neighboring Walker property because of the huge live oak trees that had grown there for over a hundred years. He'd always loved paint horses, ever since watching reruns of *Bonanza* with his grandfather. The character Little Joe rode a paint.

One day, Rebel Ranch would be divided into seven parcels and Quincy had already staked the land he wanted. His mother and brothers had agreed. So after long days working on the ranch, he then took care of his horses. He had a registered stud and five mares, but one day he hoped to have a larger operation. For now it was just a hobby.

At the sound of hooves pounding against the dry, hard ground, he swung around to see Jenny ride in bareback on the black-and-white paint horse he'd given her for her birthday. She loved the paints, and helped him all the time. They'd become close friends, but it had turned into much more for him.

Jenny slid off the horse in one easy, fluid movement. With long dark hair and riveting dark eyes, inherited from her mother, who was part Italian, she was every man's dream of the girl next door: beautiful, smart and funny. And blessed with a friendly disposition that endeared her to everyone, especially Quincy.

"Is it true?" Her eyes sparkled with high energy.

He mentally snapped to attention. "You'll have to be more specific." He knew exactly what she was talking about, but he was stalling for time.

"Is Paxton engaged?"

And there it was. Jenny and Paxton, Quincy's younger brother, had been an item since high school. Their on-and-off relationship had been the talk of Horseshoe for over a decade. Jenny wanted a home and family. Paxton favored the rodeo circuit and any pretty thing he could find. Quincy had never understood why Jenny put up with Paxton's many affairs. It was none of his business, though. Other than the fact that he'd been in love with her for years.

Quincy just wished she had asked someone else besides him. It wasn't his place to tell her about the new woman in his brother's life. But again, he and Jenny had grown close over the years and she considered him a friend, as he did her. His feelings were his own.

His hand tightened on the horse's reins. "That's what I hear." Hawk sidestepped, snorting. Quincy needed to unsaddle his horse.

"When did this happen?"

"I don't know. Mom just told us Paxton had called and said he was engaged."

"To whom?"

"I don't know, Jenny. You'll have to talk to Paxton about that. I'm not the person you should be asking."

"Don't you think I've tried? I've called and texted him and he doesn't respond. Why would he do this?" The pain in her voice twisted Quincy's insides. He'd never understood how she could keep clinging to a relationship that was so one-sided.

"Haven't you been broken up about two

months now?" He hated to be blunt, and there was nothing as blunt as the truth.

She slid her hands into the back pockets of her jeans, stretching her blouse taut across her full breasts. He looked away.

"Yes. But he always calls and we get back together."

"I guess he met someone else." He stroked Hawk, calming him, and searched for a way to end the conversation.

"A buckle bunny who fawns all over him." Her pain echoed in her voice.

He had no words to soothe her wounded pride. "I don't know. All I know is what my mother told us."

Her glistening eyes stared at him and this time he couldn't look away. "I heard there's an engagement party here on Saturday night."

Nothing in Horseshoe, Texas, stayed a secret for long. This was faster than usual, though. "That's what I've been told."

She turned toward her horse. "If Paxton doesn't answer my calls by then, I'll be coming to the party."

"It's by invitation only," he reminded her.

"Miss Kate won't care if I come."

His gut tightened like a cinch on a saddle and his nerves kept applying the pressure. He didn't want to hurt her, but she left him no choice.

"Mom would rather it be a fun evening. Please don't embarrass yourself by showing up. It would only cause tension."

"Embarrass myself?" With a twist of her head, she tossed her long, tangled hair back in anger. "Everyone in Horseshoe is talking and what they're saying is she waited all these years and he's marrying someone else. That's embarrassment, Quincy. And I can take the tension."

"Don't do it, Jenny. It will only hurt you."

"As if I'm not hurt now? He's going to tell me to my face that he's fallen in love with someone else."

"He's engaged. I think that pretty well says it all."

She fixed her heated gaze on him. "You think it's okay what he's done to me?"

"You broke up with him," he told her. "You always break up with him because it bothers you that he sees other women while he's on the circuit."

"I thought he would change," she murmured, almost to herself.

"Let it go, Jenny. It's time for you to move on."

"How do I do that, Quincy? I spent half my life waiting for him to grow up and want the same things that I do. I guess…"

He wanted to take her in his arms and hug her, because he knew things were only going to get worse. She'd lost Paxton and she didn't want to face that, but in reality, she'd lost him a long time ago. She just hadn't realized it until now.

"Hawk is getting restless. I have to unsaddle him," he said instead.

"When will Paxton be home?"

He shook his head. "Jenny, I honestly don't know."

"The party's tomorrow night so he has to come in sometime soon."

"You're not going to let this go, are you?"

"Not on your life." She vaulted onto the horse. "At the very least, Paxton owes me an explanation."

He caught the reins of her horse before she could gallop away. "Don't come to the party, Jenny. If you care anything about the Rebel family, you'll stay away and not make a scene."

"I thought you were my friend."

"I am. That's why I'm trying to protect you and keep you from getting hurt any further."

"I can take care of myself."

He loved many things about Jenny, but her stubbornness wasn't one of them. "Mom said

Paxton and his fiancée are going to stay at the ranch for a while so she can get to know the family. Maybe it would be best if you didn't come around during that time."

Her face crumpled. "You're asking me not to come to the ranch anymore?"

He drew a deep breath. "Yes. I appreciate your help with the paint horses…"

"Since Paxton rejected me, the whole family now has rejected me. I love working with the horses and you're taking that away from me, too."

There was a limit to how much Quincy could endure and this was just about the last straw. He had to end this conversation one way or the other. "Jenny—"

"Stuff it!" she shouted and jerked the reins, charging out of the barn for the Walker property, stirring up the heat and dust.

Clyde Walker, Jenny's dad, owned about a hundred acres that cut into Rebel Ranch. John

Rebel had tried to buy it for years, as had Quincy's mom, but Clyde was hanging on to his property.

Jenny lived so close, and she was like one of the family and was at the ranch a lot. Sometimes to see Paxton and other times just to ride the paint horses. Lately, Quincy had spent more time with her than Paxton. Looking back, he could see that wasn't a good idea. But it was a little late to change now.

She'd be angry and hurt for a while and then he would apologize for hurting her feelings. At this time, though, he didn't have any other choice. Maybe it was for the best. He had no future with Jenny. She belonged to his brother.

"She was pretty mad," Jude said from the doorway.

Quincy turned toward his brother. "Yeah. Paxton didn't tell her he's getting married."

"Why did you discourage her from coming to the party?"

"How do you think she's going to feel when she sees him with another woman? I'm just trying to save her some pain."

"Jenny and Paxton are adults and it's their relationship. Let them sort it out."

"Says the man who never interferes and minds his own business."

"You bet. Ready to get those broken bales of hay off the field?"

"Yeah, sure. I was just unsaddling Red Hawk."

Zane, Jude's son, ran into the barn. "Hey, Uncle Quincy, I'm going to drive the tractor."

"You got it. I'll be right with y'all."

Zane had just turned twelve and he was a clone of his father in looks—in personality, not so much. Jude and Paige, Jude's girlfriend, had gotten pregnant in high school, similar to his older brother, Falcon, and his wife, Leah. Paige was incredibly smart and had received a scholarship to the University of California, Berkeley. She was torn about what to do. In the end, her future was more important than the child she carried. They'd decided to give the baby up for adoption. But Jude hadn't been able to live with that decision. He'd gone back to the clinic and got his son and raised him. Jude hadn't seen Paige since, nor did she know about Zane.

Quincy knew that weighed heavily on his brother's mind. Jude was the quiet, responsible one in the family. He stayed mostly to himself, never caused trouble and was a straight-up kind of guy. He was the one everyone could depend on and trust. He carried a scar on his forehead where Ezra McCray had shot him the day John Rebel had killed Ezra. That, too, weighed on his mind.

It didn't take them long to get the broken bales of hay off the field. Zane drove, and Jude and Quincy threw them onto a trailer in heaps. Quincy would use the hay to feed his paints. They already had three barns full of square bales and many round bales stored away. Since it was the beginning of September, hay-baling season was almost over.

Zane drove the tractor into Quincy's barn, and Quincy and Jude jumped from the trailer to unload.

"Sorry, Quincy." Jude removed his hat to shake hay from his hair. "We have to meet Zane's teacher in less than an hour."

"Aw, Dad."

"I got it," he told his brother. He welcomed the work, anything to get his mind off Jenny.

Just as he started to stack the hay, Elias and Jericho walked in.

Quincy straightened. "Is all hay off the ground?"

"Yes, sir." Elias saluted. Of the seven brothers, Elias had a devil-may-care attitude that came with a dose of spit-in-your-eye.

Jericho grabbed a pitchfork. "I'll help you stack."

Jericho had saved his brother Egan's life in

prison and for that Kate Rebel had offered him a job. He was Egan's friend, but now he was a friend of the family. They didn't know much about Jericho, nor did they need to. He had more than proved himself to the family.

He stood about six-four and was an imposing character with dark features, long hair tied into a ponytail at his neck and a scar slashed across the side of his face. No one knew his nationality, but Egan said he was part white, black, Mexican and Indian. He'd grown up on the streets of Houston, involved in gangs and drugs. Today Quincy would trust the man with his life and the lives of his brothers. He had completely turned his life around.

Elias grabbed a pitchfork, too. "Can you believe ol' Pax's getting married? A bull must have dumped him on his head. Why get married when he has the pick of every pretty buckle bunny on the circuit?"

Quincy worked without answering. He didn't want to have this discussion.

"And Jenny? I wonder if he's told Jenny."

"That's none of our business."

Elias leaned on the pitchfork. "There's going to be fireworks, I tell you. Jenny Walker is not going to take this without a fight and I have a front-row seat. Oh, yeah. I see a catfight in Pax's future."

Again, Quincy didn't respond. They finished unloading the hay and Quincy started to jump onto the tractor to take it back to the equipment shed, but Jericho stopped him.

"I got it, Quincy. Mr. Abe is probably waiting on his supper."

"Thanks, Rico."

As Rico drove the tractor and trailer from the barn, Quincy brushed hay from his clothes. It stung down the back of his shirt and clung in sweat-slick places. He needed a shower.

"I'll see you at the house," he said to Elias.

He and Elias lived with their Grandpa Abe, who was getting up in years and at times appeared to be a little senile. They refused to let him use the stove anymore because he'd set the house on fire twice. These days Grandpa was happy to let Quincy or Elias do all the cooking. Eden, Falcon's daughter, helped out when she could.

There were four houses on the property. Their mother, Jude and Zane lived in the big two-story log house at the front. Falcon's wife had returned after many years, and they now lived in the old family home where Quincy, Elias and Egan used to live. Falcon and Leah had wanted their own house, so the brothers had happily relocated to Grandpa's. Egan had gotten married and moved out. Now Quincy and Elias were left to deal with the old man.

Grandpa's place wasn't far from the old house, and then there was the bunkhouse where Paxton, Phoenix and Jericho lived. They had a commune right there in Texas. The thought brought a smile to his face and he wasn't in a smiling mood.

So many women in the world and he had to fall in love with the one woman he couldn't have. The only way to get over it was to stay away from Jenny. And he planned to do just that.

QUINCY OPENED THE gate in the old chain-link fence and walked up the steps of the white-board house his grandfather had built for his wife many years ago. It had been redone over the years and held many memories.

Mutt, Grandpa's dog, wasn't on the front porch to greet him. Quincy couldn't remember how old the dog was, but he now had arthritis and didn't leave the yard. He was an outdoor dog and only came inside when it was cold. And he didn't like it then. He had a bed on the front porch and the back.

Opening the front door, he heard the TV. Loud. Grandpa was losing some of his hearing. He sat in his recliner, Mutt on his lap, watching an old Western.

Grandpa, with thinning gray hair, stooped shoulders and bowlegs, was about the orneri-est character you'd ever want to meet. But he was fiercely loyal and devoted to his grandsons, as they were to him.

"What's wrong with Mutt?"

Grandpa stroked the small black-and-white mixed breed dog. "I guess he's just lonely."

Quincy felt a tug on his heart, for he knew that was Grandpa's way of saying he was lonely. He usually spent time with them on the ranch, but today he'd been absent. Maybe Grandpa was feeling bad.

"Are you okay?"

"Healthy as a horse," Grandpa replied. "I knew you'd be tired so I put baked potatoes in the oven and there's steaks in the sink you can do on the grill."

"Thanks. I'll take a shower first. I'm sweaty and I've got hay all over me."

"Suit yourself. Where's Elias?"

"He's on his way."

"He better hurry up. Those potatoes'll be ready in ten minutes."

Grandpa was in an unusual mood this evening. It wasn't like him to plan supper. On second thought, Quincy went into the kitchen to check on things. The potatoes, wrapped in aluminum foil, were sitting on top of the stove. Quincy shook his head, placed them inside and turned on the oven. The steaks were thawing in the sink. That was good.

After taking a shower and changing clothes, he seasoned the steaks and placed them in the refrigerator and then went outside to the back porch to clean the grill.

He kept waiting for Elias to show up, but as

usual, Elias was dragging his heels. Quincy sat in the living room with his grandfather watching the Western. Suddenly, Grandpa turned off the TV.

"What do you think about Paxton?" Grandpa asked.

Not again. Why was everyone asking him that question?

He rubbed his hands together. "None of my business."

Grandpa pointed a finger at him. "You need to find yourself a woman."

Quincy groaned. This was Grandpa's standard lecture to his grandsons. Find a woman, get married, have babies and be happy. Sometimes it just didn't happen like that.

"And not Jenny Walker," Grandpa added for effect, and he had Quincy's attention.

He didn't know, did he? He couldn't.

His eyes narrowed. "Why do you say that?"

"She's over here all the time and it's not to

see Paxton, because he's not here. She comes to see you."

"She likes the paints and she's good with them. I don't have a problem with that because I'm busy on the ranch."

"Not all the time, so don't fool yourself, boy. I've seen the way you look at her, and that's just asking for trouble. You're a Rebel and you never cross that line. There's a lot of lines us Rebels have crossed, but we don't go after our brothers' girlfriends. Not even if they're an ex."

Elias stomped in, preventing Quincy from answering, and he was grateful for that small act. For the first time, he didn't know how to respond to his grandfather. He thought he'd kept his secret hidden. If his grandfather could gauge his feelings about Jenny, how many other family members had?

Did they all know he loved Jenny Walker?

Chapter Two

Jenny sat on the back stoop watching a cow stick her head through the barbed-wire fence to reach the green grass in the yard that Jenny had watered. The grass was always greener on the other side. That was how Paxton felt. He'd found someone better than Jenny and she had to bite the bullet and accept it.

The back door opened and her sister, Lindsay, sat down beside her. "What are you doing out here? It's hot."

Jenny was so upset, she hadn't even noticed her skin felt as if she'd taken a bath in honey.

Sticky. All she was aware of was the hollow ache in her stomach. "Thinking."

"Come on, Jenny. You have to have seen this coming. You haven't heard from Paxton in months."

"Seven weeks. That's how long it took him to fall in love with someone else."

"You have to get past this. There are a lot of guys out there who would be more than eager to go out with you."

"I've spent half my life waiting for Paxton and now I just feel like a horse without a bridle. I'm free, but I don't know which way to turn without Paxton."

"This isn't like you. What else is going on?"

The cow pushed on the barbed wire and Jenny was afraid the fence would break. She got up to shoo her away. When something around the ranch broke, Jenny and Lindsay were the ones to fix it. Their dad had had a tractor accident some years ago and now had a gimpy leg and walked with a cane. He still had cattle, but some things were hard for him to do, and having no sons, his daughters picked up the slack.

She and Lindsay were both nurses and worked in a hospital in Temple. Lindsay was director of nursing and didn't work on the floor anymore. Her job was stressful and she spent a lot of hours at the hospital, including weekends if there was a problem.

Jenny was a pre-op nurse, the one who prepared a patient for surgery, took vitals, dealt with consent forms, started an IV, calmed nerves and answered questions. Working three twelve-hour days was a challenge, but it gave her a lot of free time at home with her dad. Sometimes she was called back for extra duty. Since Lindsay was in charge, that didn't happen too often.

She resumed her seat by her sister.

"You didn't answer my question."

Jenny shrugged. "I forgot what it was."

"You're really down about something other than Paxton. What is it?"

They were four years apart and very close, and Jenny knew she could talk about anything with Lindsay. But her sister tended to be bossy and sometimes that grated on Jenny's nerves. She needed to talk, though. She wiped the palms of her hands down her jeans. "I went over to talk to Quincy to see if he knew anything about Paxton and the engagement."

"And?"

Jenny swallowed. "He was rude to me."

"What?" She poked Jenny in the shoulder. "Get out of here. That doesn't sound like Quincy. You probably were just upset and misunderstood him."

"No. It was very clear what he said."

"And what would that be?"

"He said that Paxton's fiancée was going to be staying for a while and it would be best for everyone if I didn't come back to Rebel Ranch."

"You're joking."

"I wish I was."

"After all the work you put in on his horses—for free, I might add—he's got some nerve."

"I'll have to return White Dove."

"The paint he gave you? You love that horse."

The ache in Jenny's chest ballooned into something she didn't understand. All she knew was that it hurt that Quincy had treated her as he never had before. She couldn't keep the horse he'd given her for her birthday. A birthday that Paxton had forgotten. Funny, how that little detail still stung. She would have to find the strength to return the horse.

"Keep her. Quincy would want you to have White Dove, unless he asked you to return her."

"No, he didn't say that, but it's clear I'm not welcome at the ranch anymore."

"Let me get this straight. Are you upset that someone is taking your place with Paxton? Or are you upset that Quincy asked you not to return to Rebel Ranch?"

Jenny didn't know, and that was why she was so confused and conflicted. She'd expected some consolation from Quincy, someone to understand how she felt. But what was she expecting? That he would side with her over his family? That was insane. The Rebels were fiercely loyal.

Lindsay got to her feet. "Let's go check the water troughs and then we'll open that bottle of wine we've been saving and toast good ol' Paxton and his new love. Ten bucks she's a blonde with fake boobs."

A smile tugged at Jenny's lips. Her sister sometimes had a fun side. Getting to her feet, she said, "You're on. But we'll probably never get to see her."

"Yeah. That's probably best."

Was it? Like Quincy had said, Jenny just couldn't let it go. She had to see Paxton face-to-face to end this relationship that had existed for over fifteen years. She couldn't end it by just walking away. That wasn't in her nature. Paxton Rebel was going to deal with her one way or another, and she didn't care if Quincy liked it or not.

QUINCY DIDN'T SLEEP MUCH. His mind was caught in a vortex of Paxton's crazy life, and like Grandpa had said, there were some things a brother didn't do. Tortured by his own feelings, he got up at five to help Falcon, Egan and Jericho put meat on the pit for the barbecue that evening.

His mom had invited all of Paxton's friends from high school and some from the rodeo circuit. It was going to be a big night. Quincy was hoping he could slip away for a while and miss the whole thing. That would be his kind of party.

About midmorning, he and Elias set up tables and chairs on the large deck off the den. His mom and Falcon were busy in the kitchen. Falcon was making his special barbecue sauce.

Eden and Rachel, Egan's wife, put tablecloths and votive candles on the tables. Quincy wondered where the bride-to-be was. She and Paxton had come in late last night, but no one had met her except their mother. He supposed she was sleeping in.

He and Elias were headed to the kitchen when they heard a feminine voice.

"Is anyone here?"

Quincy looked to the top of the stairs, as did Elias. A tall blonde stood there in white shorts and a bright green top that barely covered her ample breasts. Long, straight blond hair flowed down her back. *Model* flashed across his mind, like a woman in one of those lingerie catalogs. Paxton's fiancée was gorgeous.

"Damn, is that her?" Elias asked. "I think I just met my fantasy."

She floated down the stairs as if she was on a runway. Stopping two steps from the bottom, she held out her hand. "Hi, I'm Lisa Garber. Paxton's fiancée."

Elias removed his hat and bowed from the waist. "It's a pleasure, ma'am. I'm Elias, Paxton's brother."

"Yes, Paxton said he had six brothers."

"And you'll get to meet every one of us."

"I'm so excited," she gushed like a little girl. "I've never been on a ranch and I can't wait to meet everyone."

Elias thumbed toward Quincy. "This here's Quincy, another brother."

Lisa fanned her face. "My, so many handsome brothers. What's a girl to do?"

"Nice to meet you," Quincy said, and wondered what it was about the woman that annoyed him. It didn't take long for him to figure it out. Her voice, sort of a sugary squeal that could get real tedious. When a woman looked like Lisa, though, the voice didn't matter. He was sure Paxton would agree.

"Have you seen Paxton?" she asked.

"Isn't he upstairs with you?" Elias nodded upstairs.

Lisa leaned over and whispered, "Your mother wouldn't let us sleep together in her house. That's really old-fashioned, but Paxton said we had to follow her rules and I didn't want to make waves. I really missed my Teddy Bear."

Elias laughed before he could stop himself and then coughed and tried to cover it up.

"I'm sure he's at the bunkhouse," Quincy told her.

"Oh, is that where the cowboys live?"

"Sort of."

Quincy had a suspicious feeling Paxton hadn't told this woman a thing about his life, except that he was a rodeo cowboy who lived in Texas on a big ranch.

Paxton came through from the kitchen, interrupting the conversation. Quincy and Elias stared. It wasn't often they saw Paxton dressed up. He wore starched jeans and a white starched shirt and his hair was slicked back. Quincy could swear he smelled cologne.

A fun and exciting bull rider, and a ladies' man to boot, Paxton could smooth talk any woman into anything he wanted.

"Hey, babe." He took Lisa into his arms and they shared a long kiss.

"There's a bedroom upstairs," Elias said with a snicker in his voice.

Paxton turned to them. "Quincy, talk to Mom about her rules. I don't want to sleep away from Lisa."

Quincy shrugged. "Her house. Her rules. You can always sleep in the bun—"

"That's okay," Paxton cut him off, and Quincy knew his brother had definitely not told Lisa where he really lived. But that wasn't his problem and Quincy was going with his plan to get away from the party as soon as he could.

As he walked toward the kitchen, he thought Paxton had traded something real for something fluff. But then Paxton always went for the looks. Beautiful women gravitated toward him and he took advantage of that. Jenny was beautiful in a natural, sweet way that would last a lifetime. It was a shame Paxton couldn't see that.

His mom made sandwiches for lunch and introduced Lisa to the family. Quincy went back to the house to check on Grandpa, needing to get away from the circus.

"You have to wear your white shirt tonight, Grandpa."

"Fiddle-faddle. I can wear what I want."

"Mama wants everyone to look nice."

"Then, I really will wear whatever I please."

His mom and Grandpa didn't get along, which was a source of tension for the whole family.

Quincy hoped his grandpa would comply, but that was like whistling Dixie in Bangor, Maine. No one was listening or cared.

The day passed quickly and Quincy made several trips to the house to help his mother, as did all his brothers. The food was ready and the tables were set. Now they waited for the guests to arrive. Quincy even managed to get Grandpa into his white shirt and nice boots. Quincy also wore his best duds.

Eden and Phoenix were in charge of music and had the stereo blaring loudly in the den. Falcon's wife, Leah, his daughter, Eden, and Egan's wife, Rachel, had decorated the house, and everything looked festive with streamers, balloons and candles. Guests started to arrive and his mother, Paxton and Lisa went to the front door to greet them.

Although Quincy was busy handing out drinks, he kept one eye on the door, hoping Jenny wouldn't make an appearance. Phoenix was up to his usual tricks in the den. After supper, he rolled back the area rug and he and Eden started dancing. Paxton and Lisa joined them.

Before the crowd got too noisy, his mother called everyone to attention and welcomed Lisa into the family again. They clapped and cheered and Phoenix turned up the music. The party was on.

Quincy was serving beers to some rodeo guys when he noticed Jenny at the front door. His heart sank. This wasn't good. Paxton and Lisa were dancing close together to a slow number and Phoenix, Eden and Zane were clapping and cheering. Jenny, in jeans and boots, a look on her face Quincy had never seen before, walked straight toward them.

His mother motioned to Quincy and Quincy groaned inwardly. Why was this his battle? Being a dutiful son, he walked toward his mother.

"Do something," she whispered. "Jenny doesn't need to be here. She's going to get hurt."

"Mom, I don't know what I can do."

She gave him one of those looks he knew well.

"Okay."

The music stopped as Jenny walked up to the couple. Paxton and Lisa drew apart and came face-to-face with Jenny.

Color drained from Paxton's face and sweat popped out on his forehead.

"I'm Jenny Walker. Congratulations." She held out her hand.

"Thank you," Lisa replied, taking the outstretched hand. "Are you a friend of Paxton's?"

"I dated him for over fifteen years."

Not a sound was heard in the room as Jenny made the declaration. Even the half-drunk cowboys went quiet. Quincy paused behind Jenny. She had a right to say what she wanted and he wasn't going to stop her.

"Oh." Lisa looked at Paxton.

"Jenny…"

"You remembered my name. How nice. It would have been nice if you'd had the guts to answer my calls and I wouldn't have had to come here."

"Jenny, this isn't the time—"

"No, it isn't. I would've had the decency to call you if I had fallen in love with someone else. It's a shame you didn't feel the same way. Fifteen years of my life I shared with you and it didn't matter." She glanced at Lisa. "You're welcome to him and I wish you a happy life."

The last word was shaky and Quincy took Jenny's elbow and led her from the room and out the front door. They stood in the sultry September heat staring at each other.

She brushed back her hair and a telltale tear appeared on her cheek. "What is she? A model or something?"

"I don't know."

Dark eyes glistening with tears glared at him. "Oh, you know. You just won't share with me anymore. And that's okay. I understand." She gulped a breath as if she'd run a mile and Quincy got a whiff of liquor.

"Have you been drinking?"

"Yeah. It took a couple of glasses of wine to get enough courage to come over here. Stupid, huh?"

The hurt on her face and in her voice cramped his gut, and all he wanted to do was hold her and let her know someone cared about her, but he couldn't do that. That line between family loyalty and his love for Jenny was getting thinner and thinner.

She raked her hands through her hair. "Oh, crap, I don't think I combed my hair."

"You look beautiful" slipped out before he thought about it.

There was an awkward pause for a second.

Then she said, "Since you're usually nice to everyone, I won't take that personally."

There was nothing he could add to that. He really shouldn't have said it in the first place.

"Now I'm going home to finish off that bottle of wine. Tomorrow is the start of the rest of my life. A life without Paxton and without the Rebel family. You don't have to worry about me coming over here and causing trouble because this will be my last visit."

"Jenny…"

"You were right. I spend too much time over here and, like I said, tomorrow I start over with a clean page and a bright smile for a new future. I'll return White Dove first thing in the morning."

"What are you talking about?"

"I can't keep the horse."

"Why? I gave her to you! And she's pregnant."

"I'm cutting all ties, Quincy." A feather of a hiccup left her throat. "And that means I can't accept the gift. I'll just leave her in the pen at the barn."

She loved the horse, and he knew this was hurting her and he didn't know how to make it better. Even though her mind was set, he couldn't accept it.

"The horse will always be yours."

"Goodbye, Quincy. I'll miss our talks."

Me, too. More than you'll ever know. More than I can ever tell you.

He wanted to tell her there was no need for her to stay away. Lisa and Paxton wouldn't always be here. That was only asking for more trouble, though. There had to be a clean break, and his feelings didn't matter. He would get over it and move on, just like she would.

As she walked into the darkness to her truck, Quincy, for the first time in his life, felt his heart break. When his dad had died, his heart had been shattered. This was a different kind of pain, something he could change, but he was bound by family loyalty and that was what was tearing him up. He was a Rebel, though, and he would survive.

Without Jenny Rose in his life.

Chapter Three

Paxton met Quincy at the front door. "Did you talk to Jenny?"

"What do you care?" Quincy walked toward the kitchen, but Paxton followed. Falcon and their mother were in the kitchen.

"What did she say?" Paxton kept on.

Quincy got a beer out of the refrigerator and twisted off the top with more force than necessary. "You have a phone, don't you, Paxton? Why don't you try using it to call her, the way you should have days ago."

"Come on, man, get off my back."

Kate Rebel turned from the sink. "Paxton,

your father and I raised you better than this. Not calling Jenny was the coward's way out, and I didn't raise cowards. Tomorrow you will go over to the Walker place and you'll apologize with your hat in your hand. Jenny has been around this ranch since you were kids and I'm really upset at the way you've treated her."

"Mom, I couldn't call her. She'd cry and I couldn't handle that. Besides, I told her when we broke up we weren't getting back together. I wasn't ever going to change and she had to accept it. That was it for me. Jenny and I were over and I didn't feel I had to call and explain when I fell in love with someone else."

Their mother wiped her hands on a dish towel. "That may be so, but you still owe her an apology."

"I'm not apologizing!" Paxton shouted. "You treat me as if I'm in grade school. I'm a grown man and Jenny and I had a relationship and we broke it off. Do you want me to call every girl I've ever dated to let them know I'm engaged?"

Falcon was sitting at the kitchen table and he rose to his feet. Quincy was on alert because he knew Paxton wasn't going to get away with talking to their mother like that. They respected their mother. Always.

"I expect you to be a man and care about other people and their feelings, especially Jenny's, since you've dated her since you were in high school. I know it's been on and off, but that was because of you." Kate shook her head. "I'm not going to talk about this anymore. You will apologize. That is my bottom line."

"I'm not apologizing," Paxton said again with anger in his voice. "And another thing, why can't I sleep in the house with Lisa? Your ideas are old-fashioned and outdated. You have to start living in the twenty-first century."

Their mother's lips tightened into a thin line. "This is my house, and you will live by my rules. If you want to sleep with Lisa, you can sleep with her in the bunkhouse, but not under my nose, in my home. That was a rule your father and I made years ago, hoping you boys would grow up with morals and integrity. If you don't respect that, you're free to leave."

"Maybe I should. You care more about Jenny than you do about your own son."

"Excuse me?"

"I've had enough of your attitude." Falcon stepped closer to Paxton. "Apologize to Mom this instant or I'm going to lay a whole lot of hurt on you. We all worked our butts off today to give you a party and this is how you thank us, by disrespecting our mother? You know better than that."

"Shut up, Falcon. You're not my father."

That was when Falcon's fist connected with Paxton's jaw. Paxton staggered backward, landed against the wall and slid to the floor. He was immediately on his feet, ready to take on his older brother, who was now head of the family.

"Falcon!" their mother cried.

Quincy got between his brothers. "Enough. Go home to Leah, Falcon. I got this." Since they still couldn't take their preemie son out around people other than family, Leah and Falcon had taken turns coming to the party. Falcon had only been here a few minutes.

Falcon turned toward the back door at the same time that Eden danced into the kitchen. "Oh, there's my daddy. Hey, Daddy, we're having a party. Oooh." Eden grabbed her head. "I'm floating." She reached for the counter.

Eden was drunk. Before Falcon could get to her, Jude came into the kitchen. "Grandpa's passed out, Quincy. You better check on him."

"What's going on in there?"

"Phoenix spiked the punch. Zane's throwing up in the bathroom and I've got to go."

Their mother threw up her hands. "Why can't

we have a party like normal people?" She went to the doorway and shouted, "Phoenix, get in here! And bring that punch bowl."

"I'm taking Eden home," Falcon said, placing his arm around his daughter and leading her toward the back door. "Let's go home to Mama, baby girl."

Eden leaned on her father. "I love Mama and Snickerdoodle. He's so sweet. I… Daddy… Oh…" Eden ran into the utility bathroom and soon they heard her retching.

Phoenix walked in with the punch bowl in his arms. Falcon pointed a finger at him. "Your ass is mine in the morning."

"What did I do?"

"You spiked the punch," his mother told him. "And now Eden, Zane and Grandpa are drunk."

"I told them not to drink it."

Kate placed her hands on her hips. "How many times have I told you not to spike the punch?"

A silly grin split Phoenix's face. "Well, Mom, I've lost track, but I haven't done it for a while. Jenny put a damper on the party and I was just trying to liven things up a little bit, to get things going again. I didn't mean to hurt anybody."

"Pour that punch down the drain. I'll deal with you later."

"I'll deal with you in the morning," Falcon said.

"You'll have to find me first," Phoenix muttered under his breath, and Quincy had to give his younger brother credit for still cracking jokes when doom was about to rain down on him. Falcon was mad and everybody knew when he was to stay clear.

Rachel entered the room, followed by Egan. She looked at Paxton, who seemed to be holding up the wall. "Lisa's looking for you."

Paxton pushed away from the wall and walked out without a word to anyone.

"What's going on?" Egan asked. "Why does Paxton have a bruise on his face?"

"I'll tell you later," Quincy said, figuring there had been enough excitement for tonight. If Egan found out Paxton had bad-mouthed their mother, Paxton would suffer another bruise on his head. Quincy was hoping he'd come to his senses and apologize before the party was over. If not, he'd have more than words for his brother.

Egan kissed his mother's cheek. "We're going home. I'll be back in the morning to help with the cleanup."

"Don't worry about that. There's enough of us here to take care of it. Spend your Sunday morning with your wife."

"Ah, Miss Kate, that's very thoughtful." Rachel hugged her mother-in-law. "We'll both be here because Egan wouldn't be happy unless he was doing his part. And if he's not happy, I'm not happy."

Gabe, their uncle and his wife, Lacey, were

the next ones to leave. Little by little, the party broke up. Since things had settled down, Quincy went to check on Grandpa, who was snoring into the sofa. He'd wake him up later. At the front door, Paxton and Lisa were saying good-bye to friends. Elias and some rodeo guys and a girl were out on the deck and Quincy could see things were getting heated. Elias was waving his arms. Quincy groaned and made his way to the deck.

"Party's over, boys," Quincy announced.

The rodeo guy glanced at Elias and then put his arm around the girl and they walked into the den.

"What's wrong with you?" Quincy asked Elias. "You're starting a fight in Mom's house?"

"I danced with his girl, so what? She didn't seem to mind."

Quincy looked toward the sky. There had to be a full moon tonight because everyone was acting crazy. "Pick up some of these cans and let's start cleaning up."

Elias downed the rest of his beer. "You're such a downer, Quincy. Do you ever have fun?"

That question was on his mind a lot lately. He was tired of being peacemaker in the family. Maybe it was time for him to let everyone handle their own problems.

"Life isn't always about fun."

Elias laughed. "After we get everything picked up, I'll take you down to Rowdy's for a beer and introduce you to someone who could change your mind in about fifteen minutes or less."

"I'm not interested in cheap sex."

"Who said it was cheap?"

"You're an idiot." Quincy went back into the den, and Lisa and Paxton were huddled together at the bottom of the stairs. Quincy could hear them as he made his way to the kitchen.

"Come on, Pax, your mom won't know a thing. When she goes to sleep, just sneak into my room. I don't understand why you didn't come last night. I don't like sleeping by myself."

Quincy sincerely hoped Paxton wasn't thinking of doing such a thing.

"Quincy." Paxton caught up to him before he reached the door. "Please talk to Mom. She listens to you."

"I can't make her change her rules. There's an easy solution to all this. Phoenix and Jericho can move into the house and you and Lisa can have the bunkhouse to yourselves. Everyone will be happy."

Paxton glanced down at his boots. "Lisa thinks I live in the house. I haven't told her I live in the bunkhouse when I'm home."

"Have you told this girl anything about yourself?"

"Come on, Quincy. You know how it is. I met her at a party after a rodeo in Los Angeles. She's an actress and I was blown off my feet by her beauty and I couldn't wait to talk to her.

When I did, it was *bam*—" he slammed one fist into the other "—love as if I've never felt it before. I wanted to spend every second with her. After two days, I asked her to marry me."

"Where do you plan to live?"

"Man, I don't know. I haven't thought it through."

"You better start thinking. She doesn't seem like a girl who would enjoy following the rodeo circuit and sleeping in the back of a truck."

"Mom would probably let us live here in the house. Lisa seems to like the house."

"After what you pulled, you'll be lucky if she still lets you live in the bunkhouse."

"I know. I lost it for a minute. I'm just nervous about everything. I've never been this nervous in my life."

Quincy felt a pang of sympathy for his brother. He'd gotten himself into a mess. "First, you need to tell Lisa about your living arrangements and talk about how she's going to fit in with you riding the rodeo circuit. There's very little work in Horseshoe for an actress. Second, you need to apologize to Mom profusely. And third, you need to apologize to Jenny."

Paxton nodded as he followed him into the kitchen and apologized to his mother. He then asked if he could sleep in the house while Lisa was here and his mother said it was okay. He would have to sleep in the bedroom downstairs next to hers. Paxton frowned, but he didn't say anything.

Quincy went to wake Grandpa, deciding it was time to let Paxton handle his own life. He had enough worries of his own. He'd hurt Jenny and that would weigh on his mind for a while. And his heart.

JENNY SAT ON the back stoop with a wine bottle in her hand. She tipped it up, taking a swig. She'd made a fool of herself tonight, and it was going to take a lot of wine to erase the memory of her standing in the Rebel den pouring out her heart to a man who really didn't care.

Daisy, the family dog, hopped up on the step and sat beside her.

"Hey, Daisy, I made a fool of myself tonight. You know that feeling like when you chase that gopher into a hole and you start digging to reach her, but that gopher is long gone? I kept digging, Daisy, hoping to find just a little bit of emotion on Paxton's face for me. There was none. And beside him stood this goddess with the most beautiful blond hair I've ever seen in my life. Can you believe that? He replaced me with a goddess."

Daisy whined as if she understood every word. Jenny took another swig from the bottle. "You know, Daisy, looking back, I've come to the conclusion that I should have *fool* tattooed on my forehead. I clung to a fantasy in my head about Paxton. He was my soul mate, my dream come true because we met in school and became the best of friends. He was there when my mom died and I was there for him when his dad passed away. We needed each other. But he was on the rodeo circuit so much and around buckle bunnies and beautiful women. A lot of temptation. I truly believed, though, that he loved me. Now, how stupid is that? You tell me, Daisy."

She drank more wine, and the beautiful blackness of the night around her felt as comforting as a warm blanket. Here, no one was gaping at her or thinking she'd lost her mind. Here, she was safe at home.

"And then there's Quincy. Good ol' Quincy. He's loyal to a fault. I thought he was my friend and would stand beside me. We've shared as much as Paxton and I have and he let me down. Bad." She drank the last of the wine and stared off into the night.

She was going to miss Quincy probably more than Paxton. She'd been waiting all her life for

Paxton to come back and she'd just realized he was never coming home to her. Big moment. Big letdown. Big realization. She was comfortable with Paxton and she'd always known he was going to disappoint her, though with Quincy it was a shock, and that was why she was sitting here drinking wine as if it was Kool-Aid. It hurt that her friend Quincy had discarded her, too. Oh, well.

"Let's go find more wine," she whispered to the dog. She stood and swayed. "Maybe not." Gingerly, she made her way inside, humming under her breath. Tomorrow started the rest of her life.

QUINCY AND ELIAS helped Grandpa up the steps and into the house. "I can walk by myself," Grandpa complained.

"Fine," Quincy said and let go. Grandpa staggered and caught the wall.

"Ready to let me help you?"

"You're a pain in my ass, but you're my favorite grandson."

"Hey," Elias said. "I'm standing right here."

Grandpa patted Elias on the shoulder. "You're my favorite grandson." Grandpa had said that to all of them at one time or another. "Let's go to Rowdy's and get a beer."

"It's after midnight and everyone is going to bed, including you, Grandpa."

"Spoilsport."

It took him ten minutes to get Grandpa in bed. He called Elias for help to remove his baggy jeans and boots. They covered him up and walked out of the room with long sighs. It was a good thing they loved the old man or they just might choke him to death. He was that ornery.

"Did I tell you boys about the time I was in love with two women at the same time?"

Quincy and Elias stopped in their tracks. Neither wanted to listen to Grandpa's stories this late, especially when he was drunk.

"Yeah, now go to sleep," Quincy said.

They waited and soon heard snoring. They high-fived. Elias went into the kitchen and got a beer and Cheez-It crackers.

"You've got to be kidding."

"What?" Elias went into the living room, picked up the remote control from Grandpa's chair, sat on the sofa and flipped on the TV. "After having to remove Grandpa's pants, I need liquor, preferably something stronger. Sadly, this is all I have."

Elias could hold his liquor better than anyone Quincy had ever met. Soon he would crash and they wouldn't be able to wake him for several hours. Quincy shook his head and went outside to sit on the porch to de-stress from the night. Mutt was asleep in his bed and didn't move.

Quincy didn't even want to think about Paxton and Lisa. That was out of his hands and he wasn't interfering. In the morning, Quincy knew Falcon would take a strip off Paxton and

Phoenix. Their behavior tonight wasn't toler-ated in the family. And Quincy would somehow try to smooth the waters between the brothers, like always.

Running his hands up his face, his thoughts of his brothers faded and they turned to Jenny. She was the bright spot in his life. He knew the days she worked and the days she was off. When she was off, he always headed home early to be with her.

She would bring beer and peanuts. They'd sit on bales of hay and watch the paints and talk. He'd shared more with Jenny than with anyone in his life. His tour in Afghanistan he shared with no one, except Jenny. After his dad had died, Quincy had joined the Army, much to his mother's distress. He'd had to get away. The ranch wasn't the same without his father. He hadn't been able to stay away, though, and after his tour he'd come home. There was no way to explain what he'd been through or what he'd seen. Jenny had just listened and that was all he needed.

Jenny's mom had died suddenly when Jenny was in high school and she'd shared her deepest feelings and sadness about that time. She'd also talked about Paxton and her fear he was never going to settle down. Quincy had never offered advice about his brother, feeling it wasn't his place. But they seemed to be able to talk about anything.

During the springtime, she was a lot of help when the mares gave birth. Since she was a nurse, she wasn't squeamish and they'd sat many a night in the barn when a mare was having a difficult time.

His life would now change, and he would be lonely again, just like when he'd returned from Afghanistan. Jenny had filled that empty place in him and it was over.

So many times he'd wanted to tell her how he felt, but he hadn't. Paxton was his brother and he would honor that, even when it hurt, like tonight. Jenny was free now and he was sure other guys would be knocking on her door. But he wouldn't be one of them.

Looking up at a million brilliant stars, he whispered, "Goodbye, Jenny Rose."

Chapter Four

Quincy woke up at seven. He was usually up earlier, but after the long day yesterday, this morning he was dragging. He headed for the kitchen to put coffee on and then he showered and changed clothes for the day. Sipping his coffee, he walked into the living room and noticed Elias was still on the sofa sound asleep, a box of Cheez-It crackers in the crook of his arm, an empty beer bottle on the coffee table.

Grandpa stomped into the kitchen in his boots, boxer shorts and a hat, no shirt, no jeans.

"Did you forget something?" Quincy asked.

"I want coffee. I have a headache."

Quincy went back into the kitchen and poured a cup for his grandpa and set it on the table. "You got drunk last night."

Grandpa's shaggy eyebrows knotted together beneath the rim of his hat. "I don't remember drinking anything but punch." He sat at the table and cradled the cup with both hands and Quincy noticed they shook a little. That bothered him. Grandpa was getting older. Quincy knew that, but at times it was hard to see and to admit when he wanted his grandpa to be the same strong figure he'd always been.

"Phoenix spiked the punch."

"What? Wait till I get my hands on him."

"You'll have to get in line. Falcon, Jude and Mom are on him at the moment because Eden and Zane got drunk, too."

"Is that boy ever gonna grow up?"

"We can only hope."

Grandpa got to his feet and stomped toward

the living room with the cup in his hands. "I'm gonna sit in my chair and vegetate today. Did you feed Mutt?"

"No, but I will."

Grandpa eased into his chair and stared at Elias. "What happened to him?"

Quincy shrugged. "Elias being Elias."

Grandpa nodded, finished his coffee and leaned back in his chair. In a few minutes, he was sound asleep again.

Quincy let Mutt into the house and fed him, putting a pill in with his food to help ease some of his arthritic pain. He left Grandpa and Elias sleeping and went to the big house to help his mom.

He found Phoenix and their mom in the kitchen. Phoenix had on rubber kitchen gloves up to his elbows.

"What are you doing?" Quincy asked.

"Cleaning the bathrooms." Phoenix scowled. "Someone vomited on the deck. You can clean that up next," their mother told him. "And as soon as Zane gets up you can clean his bathroom."

"Mom," Phoenix wailed like a little boy.

Kate turned from the sink. "Did you say something?"

"No, ma'am."

The back door opened and Phoenix immediately ran for the living room. "If that's Falcon, you haven't seen me."

Falcon walked in a few seconds later. "Where's Phoenix?"

"Why do you ask?" their mother wanted to know.

"Eden was sick again when we got home and Leah was really upset. How can he be so irresponsible?"

"I will take care of Phoenix, son." His mother had that tone in her voice they all knew well. The voice that said she was protecting her sons with everything in her, even from each other.

Falcon took a deep breath, his broad chest expanding. "I'm sorry I hit Paxton last night. Leah is upset about that, too. I shouldn't have used violence. That's not an example I want my kids to see."

"Thank you, son. I had a long talk with Paxton last night and he apologized and I forgave him. I'll work this out with Paxton and Phoenix. That's all that needs to be said."

They all knew their mother held the power, and though they respected that, there were times it was confining. Quincy was just glad everyone was thinking clearly this morning.

"I have to get back to the house," Falcon said. "Leah was up with Eden last night and I'm on baby duty this morning. You have to come over and see John, Mom. He's becoming more alert every day and he's very attached to his mother. His eyes follow her wherever she goes."

"Don't you worry, I'll be over later to play with my grandson."

Falcon walked out, but Quincy knew his acquiescence wasn't that easy. Phoenix still wasn't off the hook. His older brother would have his say one way or the other.

"Where's Paxton?" Quincy asked.

His mom stacked dishes into the dishwasher. "We had a long talk this morning and he went over to apologize to Jenny."

Quincy handed his mom coffee cups from the table, his heart beating a little faster at the mention of Jenny. He hated that, but he couldn't control it.

Egan and Rachel came in and they continued to clean up. Rachel went upstairs to check on Zane. Since she was a teacher and going to the school anyway, she picked up Zane every morning. She'd grown attached to the boy.

Phoenix came in, rubbing his shoulder. "Rachel hit me."

Egan laughed. "Rachel's the least of your worries. Wait till Falcon and Jude get hold of you."

"I've already spoken to Falcon and made it clear that there is to be no more hitting." Their mother made her opinion clear. "I will take care of Phoenix and Paxton."

"Yes, ma'am." Egan lifted an eyebrow at Quincy and he just nodded. She wanted the matter dropped, and her sons would do just that in her presence. But later was anybody's guess.

As Quincy continued to work, he wondered how things were going with Jenny and Paxton. She'd been extremely upset last night and he hoped they could forgive and part as friends. Why he hoped that, he had no idea. He just didn't want Jenny to be hurt any more than she was.

JENNY WOKE UP to pounding, and it was in her head. Loud and painful. Crap. She rolled over and pushed hair out of her eyes. What had she done? Getting drunk solved nothing.

Crawling out of bed, she grabbed her head

to stop the pain. It didn't work. Staggering out the door, she met Lindsay in the hallway. She'd been called in to the hospital with a nursing problem last night.

"You're home," Jenny muttered.

Lindsay's mouth fell open.

"What? I know I look like hell. Right?"

"Go into the bathroom and look in the mirror."

"I don't need to see myself."

"Yes, you do." Lindsay pushed her into the bathroom and Jenny stared at the wild-looking woman in the mirror. Her hair looked like a rat's nest.

"What did you do last night?"

"Uh…" The embarrassing confrontation at the party came rushing back, as did the pounding.

"Not to throw you into a tizzy or anything, but Paxton's waiting to talk to you in the kitchen."

She swung around. "Tell him I don't want to see him."

Lindsay eyed her sister, and Jenny hated it when she did that. "Don't you think it would be best to end this the right way?"

"And how would that be?"

"By being an adult and listening to what he has to say. Obviously, he wants to apologize."

"You know what he can do with that apology."

"Jenny…"

"Oh, okay." She walked out the door.

Lindsay followed her. "Don't you think you should comb your hair and change?"

"For what? I'm not dressing up for Paxton. I'm not doing anything for Paxton."

"Jenny, you're in shorts and a tank top."

Marching to the kitchen, she shut out Lindsay's nagging voice and went straight to the coffeepot. Her dad sat in his chair drinking coffee and eating breakfast. With his hat in his hand, Paxton stood there, looking nervous.

Her dad pushed away from the table and reached for his cane. "I'll give you kids some time alone, but I'll be right outside." Giving Paxton a long look, he limped out the back door.

Jenny poured a cup of coffee, wishing her head would stop pounding. She took a deep breath and turned to face Paxton. The handsome face she'd loved for so many years now had worry lines stretched across it and the stress showed in his brown eyes.

Of the brothers, Paxton and Phoenix were the only ones under six feet. Phoenix was slim while Paxton was all muscle and that did well for him as a bull rider. He was as tough as any bull he'd ever ridden, with grit and determination unequaled by any cowboy. That was one of the things she had loved about him.

She sat at the table and sipped her coffee. "Why are you here, Paxton?"

He gripped the hat in his hand. "I came over

here to apologize for my behavior. My mom said I took the coward's way out and she was right. I should've called you."

"You needed your mother to tell you that?"

"Come on, Jenny." He motioned toward the chair. "May I sit down?"

"If you must." She took a gulp of coffee, hoping it would boost her wide-awake, recharge her batteries and possibly make her a beautiful blonde.

"I'm going to be completely honest."

"Now, that would be refreshing."

"I've never lied to you, Jenny, even when you asked me about other girls, I told you the truth. The last time we broke up, I told you it was for good. We couldn't keep doing what we were doing. It wasn't working for either one of us."

She remembered how much that had hurt. But then, all their breakups had been hard. She'd just never thought…

"Can you remember the last time we had sex?"

Her eyes jerked to his. "What?"

"I can't. Can you?"

She just stared at him and resisted the urge to smack him. How dare he ask her that?

"When we were in high school, we needed each other. I was there when your mom died and you listened while I talked about my dad. We leaned on each other because we needed that support and we trusted each other. That turned into much more, but looking back, our relationship was always about friendship. When I started spending more time on the circuit and away from home, I realized there were a lot of pretty women out there who didn't want to be tied down. I never wanted to be tied down. I told you that many times, but you never seemed to hear me. You wanted so much more than I could give you."

She twisted the cup in her hand, looking down

into the dark depths and seeing that young girl who'd clung to Paxton because she'd had no one else. Her sister had been dealing with her own pain and so had her father. Paxton had soothed all those broken pieces inside her.

"Whatever we had was good and we both clung to it because it made us feel better. But that's not what real love is. I know what it is now. And when you're in love, you want to be tied down."

There was a butter knife on the table and she picked it up and handed it to him. "Why don't you just stab me in the heart?"

"Jenny, you're the best friend I ever had and I hate to lose our friendship. But I have to move on now. Please understand that. I will always remember our teenage years as something special. It made me the man I am today."

Tossing the knife onto the table, she got up to refill her cup. It was almost full, so she poured it down the drain and watched it disappear. Just like her feelings for Paxton. Or as near as they were ever going to.

She hated that everything he was saying was true. She couldn't remember the last time they'd had sex. It had been a very long time. She'd just kept clinging to the past and hoping those old feelings would come back, but they hadn't. He didn't need her anymore and she wondered why she still needed him.

"I think we clung to the past because it was comfortable for both of us, an easy place to be. But we're older and we need more, or at least I do."

She turned from the sink, determined to be the adult she was supposed to be. "I'm really trying to listen with an open heart, but it would be much easier to smack you for the hurt you've caused me."

A smile touched his handsome face. "I'll miss your humor. You always could make me smile and bring me out of the dumps better than anyone."

"So you really love this Lisa?"

"Yes. She's all I ever think about. Phoenix says I'm in lust, but I know differently."

"Do you? You once said you loved me."

He stared straight into her eyes. "How long has it been since I said that?"

And then it hit her. He hadn't said it in years. They hadn't had sex in years. They hadn't been anything in years, only in her mind. She'd been clinging to the past just like he'd said. It was comfortable and she didn't want to venture outside her comfort zone. So where did that leave her? *Alone* echoed through the hollow places of her heart.

And that was what scared her.

The moment she felt the fear inside her, it was gone, and it was replaced with something stronger—her pride. She wasn't a weepy clinging sort of woman, and she wasn't going to let him get away with making her feel like one.

"Do you remember the prom?"

He sighed. "Jenny, I don't want to relive our high school years."

"I remember the prom," she went on as if he hadn't spoken. "What a night." She leaned against the cabinet, holding on to her cup as if it would keep her rooted to the floor and her emotions in check. "We had such a good time dancing with each other and with our friends. I was dancing with Brad Coleman and you were dancing with his girlfriend, Tonya. When the music stopped, you and Tonya weren't there. Where were you, Paxton?"

"Jenny…" His sun-browned skin paled.

"Let me see, oh, yes, you were out in the foyer ramming your tongue down her throat. It was our first big fight, but being the big fool that I am I forgave you." She touched her forehead.

"I really should have *fool* tattooed there, don't you think?"

"That was my fault, but you were holding out on sex and Tonya…well… You can be a prude sometimes."

"Oh, no." She shook a finger at him. "You don't get to come over here and make me feel guilty. You're a liar, a cheater and a jerk. I hope you treat Lisa much better than you ever treated me."

"Jenny—"

"I just can't believe I spent all these years with a fantasy in my head, because that's what it was—just a fantasy."

"I'm sorry you're hurt."

"Oh, I'm not hurt anymore." She placed her coffee cup on the counter. "I'm moving on, Paxton, and that's an exhilarating feeling. There has to be a nice guy out there somewhere who appreciates fidelity and undying love." She headed for the hallway and turned back. "Thank Miss

Kate for me for forcing you to come over here and apologize. It has opened my eyes and I feel liberated. Have a good life, but I'm really skeptical that you know the difference between lust and love. That's Lisa's problem now. Hallelujah." She walked down the hall, leaving a stunned Paxton staring after her.

She raised her arms in victory. "Oh, yeah. That felt good," she murmured under her breath. Falling headfirst onto her mattress, she groaned from the pounding in her head. She hoped she remembered all this vividly when her mind cleared, and that she could easily discard her feelings for Paxton. That would be a test in the days to come. There were a lot of guys out there, and she was going to find the perfect one who would love her just as much as she loved him. Oh, God, was that another fantasy?

Were there even guys like that? The ones who believed in true love and fidelity? Of course, she told herself. It may be like finding the proverbial needle in a haystack, but she wasn't going to give up. She began to softly sing the song "I Will Survive" under her breath and drifted into sleep.

Chapter Five

Jenny slept most of Sunday in a drug-like stupor. When she was awake, it felt as if tiny people with big hammers were building a roof on her head. But even her aching head couldn't block the thought that she had wasted a lot of years on Paxton. It wasn't his fault. It was hers. She'd refused to see what even a blind person could—there was no future there.

By Monday morning, she was feeling better. Even her bruised pride had survived the weekend. She was on duty at the hospital, so she was up at 4:00 a.m. to start a twelve-hour shift, getting patients ready for surgery. And on

Mondays the schedule was usually full. Back-to-back surgeries all day long.

She'd gotten up thirty minutes earlier because she had an errand to do. Slipping on jeans, boots and a T-shirt, she hurried toward the back door and the barn. Since it was September and still hot, White Dove preferred the corral to the barn. Jenny grabbed a couple of bridles and made her way there. The black-and-white paint horse raised its head as Jenny approached and trotted to the fence, followed by Jenny's quarter horse, Sassy.

The moonlight cast an iridescent beam of brightness, making it easy for Jenny to see. She climbed the fence and stroked the horse's face. Quincy had bought her at a horse auction in Laredo. She was skittish and had marks on her coat where she'd been beaten with a whip. Quincy had said he had gotten her cheap, but she doubted that. The horse was beautiful with a black patch on her left rump extending down part of her leg. Another black patch was on her shoulder and ran down part of her leg and stomach. The area between the patches was white and to Jenny it resembled a dove. Quincy had made a face when she'd said it, but he'd named her White Dove anyway. There were other black spots on her neck and body and her face had a white blaze. She was due in the spring with her first foal.

Jenny would miss that. A tiny choke squeezed her throat. "Sorry, girl, I have to return you."

She slipped a bridle on Dovie and then on Sassy. With one hand, she opened the gate and then led the horses through and closed it. As she vaulted onto Dovie's back, she winced. She wasn't all that crazy about riding bareback, but since Dovie was pregnant Jenny wasn't putting a saddle on her. Kneeing Dovie, she started off on a well-used trail to the Rebel property, leading Sassy.

She picked her way through the woods carefully, trying not to think that this was the last time she'd be riding this horse. The light thump of hooves sounded like thunder in the quiet darkness. Only the chirp of crickets and the croak of frogs in the small pond interrupted the quiet now and then. The darkness was all around her like a comfortable jacket, and she felt safe in these woods. She'd grown up here and knew every inch of them.

The closer she got to Quincy's corral, the more she wanted to turn back. Even though her heart was breaking at having to give up something she loved, she continued her journey. That was what starting over was all about.

Soon she reached the property line and dismounted to open a barbed-wire gate she and Quincy had installed so Jenny wouldn't have to walk so far to the barn. She swung onto Dovie's back and made her way to Quincy's barn and corral. Once there, she dismounted again and led Dovie through the pipe gate.

She stroked the horse's face. "Goodbye, girl. Quincy will be good to you just like I was." Wrapping her arms around Dovie's neck, she held on tight.

The horse neighed softly.

Her throat squeezed in pain as tears threatened. Quickly, she kissed the horse and walked out, closing the gate. Dovie neighed again, but Jenny kept walking. Swinging onto Sassy's back, she rode away, letting the tears fall where they may.

As she made her way home, she refused to think about the past. It was over and she couldn't go back. Today she was starting over and that began with breaking all ties to the Rebels.

No matter how much it hurt.

QUINCY WAS UP early on Monday. It was the beginning of a workweek and they always had a family meeting to discuss what needed to be done and who was going to do it. Before going to the office, he went to feed his paints. As he carried sweet feed in a bucket to a trough in the corral, he glimpsed White Dove walking back and forth along the fence.

Damn it! Jenny, you didn't have to do this. Dovie continued to walk the pipe fence line, agitated. The other mares, sensing her anxiety, began to follow her. Red Hawk threw up his head and neighed, not liking that his mares were upset.

Quincy dumped the feed and the mares immediately trotted to the trough. Dovie continued to pace. He'd check in again on her later. A newcomer always interrupted the herd, but Dovie wasn't new. The mares and Hawk knew her. It was Dovie who was causing a disturbance and he'd have to do something about it if her behavior continued during the day.

Late getting to the meeting, he quickly found a seat and was surprised to see Grandpa present. He'd left him nursing a cup of coffee this morning.

Fall roundup was around the corner and Falcon talked about what pastures they would work first. So far, nothing had been said about Saturday night. Paxton wasn't even there and Phoenix sat slumped in a corner, probably hoping that Falcon and Jude couldn't see him.

"Today I want all the fence lines checked on the pastures to make sure once we start roundup, the cattle can't break the fences," Falcon said.

"Paxton will be spending time with Lisa," his mother announced. "And Phoenix will be helping me at the house for the next few days."

"You've got to be kidding me." Elias was the first to voice his opinion, as always. "I get to work my butt off while Paxton and Phoenix get to laze around."

Their mother looked directly at him. "Paxton has a guest and he will spend time with her. Phoenix will be making amends for what he did Saturday night. He will be cleaning the gutters on the house and anything else I find that needs doing."

"I'll switch with you, Elias," Phoenix offered.

"There will be no switching," Kate stated. "You will make amends to everyone. Poor Zane was still not feeling well this morning."

"I'm sorry."

"You better be," Jude said. "I find it very hard to understand why you do the things you do."

"To your old grandpa, too. You need to grow up, boy."

"I'm sorry, Grandpa. I'll do anything you want to make amends."

"Good. My toenails need clipping. I'll see you at my house when your mom is through with you."

Phoenix groaned and everyone else laughed. They all knew Grandpa's toenails were as hard as cement. They had to use a hoof clipper to trim them. It was usually Quincy's job and he was happy to hand off the job to his baby brother.

The meeting broke up and everyone went their separate ways. Egan and Elias went north and Quincy and Jericho went east. Jude took a flatbed trailer and went into town for supplies.

The fences were checked often so they were in pretty good shape. A couple wires needed tightening, but other than that, the fences would hold during fall roundup.

As he neared the McCray fence line, Quincy could see Gunnar and Axel, two of Ira's sons, through the weblike branches of the trees. They had a calf on the ground and Quincy and Jericho stopped to make sure it wasn't a Rebel calf.

"What do you think?" Rico asked.

"I think they're awfully close to the property line and that could possibly be one of our calves."

They rode closer and Quincy reached in his saddlebags for his binoculars. He couldn't see the brand for Gunnar's big frame, but the calf was white, and they didn't have any white calves that he could recall.

Gunnar rose and noticed them. He and Axel immediately mounted their horses and rode to the fence line. Avoiding a confrontation was always the best course of action, but Quincy wasn't running.

"What are you gawking at, Rebel?" Gunnar taunted.

Quincy nodded toward the white calf. "Just making sure that's not a Rebel calf."

"We stay clear of your mangy cows."

"Yeah, right."

The calf meandered toward the fence and Rico rode to get a closer look.

"If he crosses our fence line, he's a dead man," Gunnar said.

"Does he look stupid?" Quincy's rifle was in the saddle scabbard and he wanted to make sure he could get to it if trouble broke out. Slowly, he undid the leather tab that held it in place.

Rico rode back to Quincy. "It's not our calf."

Gunnar folded his hands over the saddle horn, eyeing Rico. "You need a bodyguard these days, Rebel?"

"Jericho?" Quincy nodded toward his friend. "Nah. He's part of the Rebel family now and the man who can make you cry 'mama' in five seconds or less."

Gunnar laughed, jerked his reins and he and his brother rode off.

"I've seen his kind in prison," Rico said. "They love to make trouble."

"Yeah." Quincy turned his horse toward home. "That's why it's best to avoid them, but sometimes they make it impossible."

It was late afternoon by the time they made it back. In the distance, Quincy could see his corral, and White Dove continuing to walk the pipe fence, looking for a way out, looking for home and Jenny. Had she been doing that all the time they'd been gone?

He pulled up, as did Rico beside him. Rico followed Quincy's gaze. "Isn't that Jenny's horse?"

"Yeah."

"She doesn't seem too happy."

"No. Tell Falcon I'll catch up to everyone later." He rode toward his barn, and Dovie didn't even stop in her quest to find a way out.

"Do you need help?" Rico asked from behind him. He should've known the man wouldn't ride away. He was always available for help. The Rebel family had been lucky to find someone as honorable and loyal as Jericho Johnson.

"Nah. I'm just going to see if she'll eat. That might calm her down."

Quincy dismounted, as did Rico. They filled the trough and the horses trotted over to eat. All of them except Dovie. Quincy jumped over the fence and slowly walked toward her. Dovie stopped and threw up her head in agitation. Her nostrils flared.

"I don't think she likes you," Rico murmured from the fence.

"Come on, girl, aren't you hungry?" He held out the feed in his hand to her. In response, she threw up her head again and pawed the ground with one hoof.

The horse wasn't bending to Quincy's will. Dovie didn't want anyone but Jenny. He walked back and jumped over the fence. Rico didn't ask many questions, but Quincy could see he had plenty to ask about why the horse was back on Rebel land.

"She can't go on without food," Quincy remarked.

"No one can."

"Jenny's one stubborn woman."

Rico looked at him. "Sorry, my friend." Again the man didn't ask questions.

"She figures since Paxton's engaged to someone else, she has to break all ties to the family."

"She was really upset on Saturday."

"Yeah, but there's nothing I can do about that."

"Isn't there?"

Quincy glanced at his friend. Rico headed for his horse. "I better check in with Falcon." After saying that, he rode away with a quiet dignity that sometimes frustrated Quincy. People needed to talk, to share. But what did he know? Talking never helped him and it had gotten him in a lot of trouble at times.

As he watched White Dove continue her protest, Rico's words came back to him. There was nothing he could do. Why would Rico say that? The obvious stared him right in the face. Rico probably knew how he felt about Jenny. He hadn't been fooling anyone. All the more reason to stay away from Jenny. But as he watched the horse kicking up dirt in anger, he thought that might not be possible.

AFTER SPENDING TWELVE hours on her feet, Jenny was beat and ready for food and rest. Lindsay had supper ready. That sounded great, but her excitement faded when she saw it was tuna casserole. Her dad loved it, but Jenny didn't care for it. She ate it anyway, but after supper, she filled a bowl with butter-pecan ice cream and went out on the stoop to enjoy her treat.

Her gaze went to the barn. The corral opened to a pasture and she could see Sassy and Lindsay's horse in the distance. No Dovie. The ice cream clogged her throat and she swallowed before tears took over. It was actually almost funny that she was going to miss Dovie more than Paxton. But then, someone had to be around for you to miss them.

During the surgeries today, there were times she would think of Paxton and wonder what had kept her hanging on for so long. What would make her so weak?

Her mother's death had hit her hard because

it had been so unexpected. She'd died in her sleep from a brain aneurysm. It had been such a shock. Jenny had been close to her mother and suddenly all that love her mother had bestowed on her had been gone and Paxton had replaced it. He was a charmer, a talker and a person who liked to touch and hug. Not many guys were like that and Jenny had soaked it up. Maybe just a little too much.

Daisy hopped up on the stoop beside her. "Hey, girl, where have you been? Chasing that gopher again?"

Daisy sniffed at the empty bowl of ice cream. "Okay, but don't tell Lindsay. You know she doesn't like you eating out of the family dishes." She placed the bowl on the stoop and Daisy licked it clean.

The screen door opened and Lindsay poked her head out. "Do you want the bathroom first?" They shared a bathroom. The house had three bedrooms and two baths. Their dad had tried to get one of them to take the master bath, but they always refused.

"Nah. I'm gonna sit out here for a while."

Lindsay spotted the bowl by Daisy. "Did you let her eat out of that bowl?"

"Why, heavens no."

Lindsay didn't buy that for minute. "You do know she licks her butt."

"So?"

"You're an idiot." Her sister came out and sat beside her. Before she could get on her soapbox, her eyes strayed to the corral. "Where's Dovie?"

Jenny swallowed. "I took her back."

"When?"

"Before I went to work."

She put her arm around Jenny. "I'm so sorry."

"Thanks."

"You were so out of it yesterday, we didn't get to talk about Paxton's visit."

"Miss Kate sent him over to apologize.

Wasn't it wonderful that his mother had to point that out?"

"Did you vent your anger?"

"You bet, and then some, but according to Paxton, our relationship ended a long time ago and it's my fault for not realizing that."

"And?"

She looked at her sister. "What?"

"How did you respond to that?"

She shrugged. "I have all these feelings inside me and I'm trying to sort them out, but every time I do, I see myself in a negative light. Why would I keep holding on to Paxton when he had clearly moved on years ago?"

"It's hard to let go of that first love."

Her sister had fallen in love in high school and her boyfriend had joined the marines and had been killed in Afghanistan. She still struggled with losing him.

This time she hugged her sister. "I would say we need another bottle of wine, but I'm off the hard stuff for a while. My head will never be the same."

"You know what they say, the best way to get over an old love is to find a new one. There's a new hot intern at the hospital. I'll introduce you."

Jenny drew back. "Introduce me? Why don't you introduce yourself?"

"Oh, he's too young for me. Besides, you're the pretty one."

Jenny laughed. "I'm the pretty one?"

Her sister nodded. "Yes. You're the pretty one and I'm the smart one."

Jenny laughed until her head hurt again.

"Stop laughing."

"Okay." Jenny sobered up. "Let me get this straight—the smart one painted her bedroom and forgot to open the windows and the fumes made her high. This same smart one has run out of gas two times in the past month because she doesn't look at the gas gauge on her car. And—"

"Okay, I get it. I'm not smart and you're not pretty. Are you happy?"

"Hell, no. You have a masters in nursing so I guess that qualifies. You're just ditzy at times and, regrettably, I'm the same way. Must be in our DNA."

"You're ditzier than me."

"Am not."

Lindsay laughed. "And you're prettier."

"You should see Paxton's fiancée."

"Big boobs, huh?"

"She looks like a model from Victoria's Secret."

Lindsay frowned. "How do you know that?"

Too late Jenny realized her mistake. "I went over there Saturday night and said my piece."

"Oh, Jenny. I should have been home to stop you."

Jenny didn't think that would have helped.

Quincy had tried and if Quincy hadn't been able convince her, no one would have.

"It's over, so let's forget about it. Today I started a new life. I forgot to tell you that."

"How's that going?"

"Seems like the same old life. Same old heart-ache."

Lindsay hugged her and got to her feet. "It'll get better. Now I'm going to take a shower and then go over some nursing data. They're not cutting my budget again."

Jenny sat on the stoop trying not to feel as if her world had come to an end. She invested so many years in Paxton and it was hard to think of her life without him. Starting over was a big plan, but the problem was, she was still Jenny with the same feelings. That wouldn't change overnight. She wondered how long it would take for her to forget her high school love.

The light was beginning to fade, but through the dimness she saw a rider coming through the woods—a rider leading a horse behind him. As he drew closer, she recognized the figure, tall and straight in the saddle. *Quincy.*

What was he doing here?

Chapter Six

It didn't take Jenny long to recognize the horse. *White Dove.* Quincy was bringing Dovie home. Her heart skipped a beat like a kid at Christmastime getting a special gift. She jumped up and ran toward them and then stopped. What was she doing? Taking a long breath, she turned and went back to the stoop. She couldn't accept Dovie and she had to have the strength to say no once again.

Effortlessly, Quincy reached down, opened the gate and pulled Dovie forward. Removing her bridle, he said something to her and Dovie trotted into the pen and straight to the water trough. Quincy watched her for a second and then he dismounted and looped his reins over the fence.

In an easy-moving sort of way, he made his way to her. He was tall, probably the tallest of the Rebel brothers. And lean—there was not an ounce of fat on his body. Not that she knew that personally. He reminded her of the actor Gerard Butler, with a steel-like demeanor wrapped around a softness that was undeniable. Quincy had a big heart and he was easy to talk to, easy to be with and—

Her thoughts skidded to a stop. She'd never thought of Quincy in that way. They were just friends. She must just be emotional and upset.

He sat beside her and suddenly the stoop was too small. She was never nervous in Quincy's presence, but today for some reason she was very aware of him as a man. He raised his knees and rested his forearms on them, not saying a word.

Finally, he asked, "How you doing?"

"So-so."

He clasped his hands together and she noticed for the first time how big they were, with long fingers that were strong and capable. Calloused hands. Gentle hands. She'd seen him break a horse with the softness of his voice and the gentleness of his touch.

"I want to apologize for what I said on Friday. I didn't mean for you to stay away from Rebel Ranch forever. I just wanted to save you the pain of seeing Paxton with Lisa."

"I can take care of myself, Quincy."

He looked at her then, his eyes dark beneath the rim of his hat. "Yeah, I'm known for sticking my nose in where it doesn't belong and I really should have stayed out of it. It was none of my business."

"I know you had good intentions, but it did hurt when you told me not to come around anymore."

He placed his hands on his knees. "Let's make this official and permanent. You're always welcome at the ranch whether you're dating Paxton or not."

"Well, as my dad would say, that old dog ain't gonna hunt no more. Paxton and I are over. For good. And I won't be coming back to Rebel Ranch, but thanks for the invitation. That means a lot." It meant more than she could tell him, because deep in her heart she knew her friend hadn't let her down. Her chest suddenly felt lighter.

"Paxton and Lisa won't always be there. I think they're leaving at the end of the week."

She reached out and touched his arm and wished she hadn't. Solid muscle and bone vibrated along her fingertips. All male. It was tempting and a little disconcerting she'd noticed that, and she drew her hand away as if she'd touched something hot. Something hot in a good way.

"That doesn't make any difference. I'm rebuilding my shattered life and I can't step back into the past and do that."

"How's that working out?"

She made a face. "It's still the same old life. If I dyed my hair blond, do you think it would make a difference?"

"To what?"

"To moving on. Lindsay says there's a hot new intern at the hospital and I might just try my luck with a new look and a new beau."

Dusk settled in and the heat of the day loosened its grip. From the porch light, she could see the chiseled lines of his face clearly and the frown that marred it. "To get back at Paxton?"

"No. To regain my confidence."

"Jenny, give it some time and you'll land on your feet."

"Not always. You remember that time you were breaking that horse and I was sitting on the fence watching? You said to slip onto her back so she could feel the weight of a rider, which I did. She bucked me right onto my butt."

"But I was there to catch you."

"Yeah." Quincy was always there, and suddenly the breath in her lungs felt heavy and she had trouble breathing. Quincy was always there with his gentle hands and loving spirit. *Quincy was always there.* She cleared her throat as emotions she didn't understand swamped her. Gazing toward the corral, she asked, "Why did you bring Dovie back?"

"She was causing a problem."

"What do you mean?"

"She was walking the fence line and not eating, and I don't think she drank anything all day. Look at the way she's drinking water. She was staging a protest. She wanted to come home, so I brought her."

A lump formed in Jenny's throat, but she quickly brought her emotions under control. "Don't give me that. You're very good with horses and I know you could've talked her into a better mood. She would've settled down eventually."

"She's pregnant and I didn't want to chance it. She actually refused feed out of my hand, and I knew that was a bad sign, so I did the only thing I could. I brought her to the one person she wants to be with."

"I can't keep her," she murmured.

"I can't take her back because she's disruptive to the other mares, even to Red Hawk. If the mares got into a hoof-kicking fight, I'm afraid I might lose a foal. And I'm going to be away over the weekend so I needed to do something now."

Quincy had a lady friend in Plano, and he went there quite often. He never spoke about her to Jenny, and she never asked, but now she was very curious. It was none of her business, she reminded herself, and quickly focused on what he was saying.

"I've seen you do amazing things with horses and I'm not buying any of this."

"It's the truth. If you bring her back, I'll have to sell her. We're starting roundup and I don't have time to deal with the situation."

"You're kidding." She brushed back her long brown hair and suddenly realized she was skimpily dressed in shorts and a spaghetti-strap tank top and no shoes. Feeling self-conscious and vulnerable, she drew up her knees and wrapped her arms around them. Her emotions were all over the place.

"No. I'll have to sell her."

Before she could stop herself, she slapped his arm. "Don't you dare." Then she realized what he was doing, playing on her love for the horse. She shook a finger at him. "Oh, no, you don't."

He caught her finger and entwined his fingers with hers. At the touch of his calloused hands, tiny sparks of electricity shot through her, making her very aware of how attractive Quincy was. She wanted to keep touching him.

She cocked an eyebrow. "You're sneaky and crafty."

"Whatever works with a stubborn woman."

She laughed. She couldn't help herself. His sweet, loving nature was winning her over and she was tired of fighting. She could keep Dovie, so she didn't see the harm.

"Deal?"

"Deal."

He tightened his hand on hers and her breath caught for a moment before he let go. She didn't understand why she was so attracted to Quincy now. It had to be a rebound thing and she would be careful not to read too much into it.

"But…" Starting over didn't include renewing her friendship with Quincy, even as much as she wanted to. She had to leave the Rebels in her past. "I still can't come back to Rebel Ranch."

Resignation pinched the corners of his mouth. "If that's the way you want it."

A long, hot breath burned her throat. "It is."

He stood and strolled away without another word. *A slow-moving, sweet-talking man* ran through Jenny's mind. A handsome sweet-talking man, she amended, and then shook her head to clear it of another fantasy. There was no future in loving a Rebel man. She'd learned that the hard way.

QUINCY MOUNTED HIS horse and rode away. Pulling up, he looked back and saw Jenny in the corral hugging Dovie. She was happy. The horse was happy. All was well again and he headed home.

Jenny was right. He could've settled the horse down, but he didn't see a reason to do that when she didn't belong at the ranch anymore. Taking her back to Jenny was the logical solution. Breaking all ties might not be an option for him or for her. But their time together would be less and less, and soon maybe all the memories would dim and she would move on and so would Quincy.

On Saturday, he'd go see Wendy and spend the weekend. That always made him feel better, and he'd return with a new perspective on his future.

It was completely dark when he rode into the big barn and dismounted. He unsaddled Aries and took care of him before going to the house.

He stopped short as he opened the screen door. Grandpa lay back in his recliner and Phoenix was on his knees, clipping Grandpa's toenails with a hoof trimmer, or at least he was trying to.

When Phoenix saw Quincy, he jumped to his feet. "Thank heavens you're home. I can't do this. You have to."

Quincy shook his head and walked into the kitchen. "I didn't spike the punch."

"Come on, Quincy." Phoenix followed him. "My stomach's not that strong."

Quincy almost gave in. Almost. "Sorry, you play, you pay."

"Doesn't anybody on this ranch know how to have fun?"

"I don't call it fun when you get your grandpa, your niece and your nephew sick."

Phoenix held up his hand as if he was going to place it on the Bible. "I promise to never spike the punch again."

"That doesn't sound too sincere."

"What do you mean? It's been an awful day for me. I had to clean out gutters, mow the yard and weed the flower beds. Tomorrow, Mom said I had to work in the garden. I'd rather ride a bucking bull any day of the week than do work like that."

"Then, don't spike the punch."

Phoenix groaned.

Quincy noticed the big pot on the stove. "What's that?"

Phoenix shrugged. "I don't know. Grandpa had me put it on. Something like a crawfish boil, except it doesn't have any crawfish, just sausage, potatoes, corn and onions, and Grandpa put all kinds of seasoning in there." He leaned over and whispered, "I wouldn't eat that if I were you. It'll probably blow a hole in your stomach."

"Get in here and finish my toenails, Phoenix!" Grandpa called.

Phoenix looked at Quincy with hope in his eyes, but Quincy shook his head, figuring this was a lesson Phoenix had to learn. With slumped shoulders, Phoenix went back into the living room.

Elias came through the back door laughing. He sailed his hat toward the hat rack and it landed perfectly.

"What's so funny?" Quincy asked.

"Paxton and Lisa were in the barn when I rode in. Paxton's got him a girl who's afraid of horses. Oh, man. That's hilarious. He wanted to take her for a moonlight ride, but she wasn't having any of it. She wasn't liking the barn too much, either. It smells—" he dropped his voice to a squeal "—and it's dirty and primitive." Elias shook his head. "Our brother has himself a problem. They were going into town, probably to find a motel. Paxton's getting a little deprived. Oh, man, I love it." With a hot pad, he lifted the lid from the pot. "What's this?"

"Supper."

"Whatever. I need a shower."

Elias went toward the bathroom and Quincy wondered what Paxton was going to do about a woman who hated horses. He spent half his life on one. With Paxton's charm, he could talk her around. Life was full of surprises and this wasn't a good one for Pax, who rode bulls and roped for a living. But it wasn't Quincy's problem.

As always, his thoughts turned to Jenny. She'd forgiven him, or at least she'd seemed to. And what did it matter? He was never going to see her again. She was moving on with the new intern and that wasn't going to bother him because that's the way it had to be—to keep family harmony.

As EACH DAY PASSED, Jenny's broken heart began to mend. She called Miss Kate and apologized for interrupting the party. The woman was very gracious and apologized for her son's bad manners. Jenny thought she should also apologize to Lisa, but she just couldn't bring herself to go to Rebel Ranch again. Instead, she asked Miss Kate to convey her apologies to the woman. And that put an end to that horrible weekend.

She met the new intern and they went out on a date. Mr. Hot turned out to be Mr. Boring. At dinner, his favorite conversation was himself and his big plans for the future. He was handsome, though, with blond hair and beautiful blue eyes, but there was just no way to get past the boring part. So she decided to give the dating route a rest for a while.

She missed riding the paints, and every day she thought more and more about it and wondered who was riding them for Quincy. He probably did it after work. With his schedule, that would be hard. His grandfather took up a lot of his time and he wouldn't change a minute of that. Even though he had six brothers, Quincy took on that responsibility without a second thought. That was the kind of person he was. At the oddest times, she'd discover herself thinking about him and she found that strange, since she'd stopped thinking about Paxton. Almost.

After that first week, and realizing their relationship had been over for a long time, Jenny's pain lessened, as did her thoughts of Paxton. Her happy time was taking care of Dovie. She couldn't wait to see how the foal would turn out, since Red Hawk was chestnut-red-and-white and Dovie was black-and-white. Jenny watched her closely in case of problems.

She and Lindsay planned to cull the herd in October to cut down on feeding during the winter months. They would take a week of their vacation to do that. The good thing about forgetting the past was that Jenny was busy and she didn't have a lot of time to mope. But if there was any moping done, it dimmed with each day. She grew stronger and confident and no one was ever going to take her pride again.

BY THE END of the week, as Quincy had predicted, Paxton finally got Lisa on a horse. She wasn't crazy about it, but they were working out their problems and Quincy thought that was good.

Quincy was saddling Aries for the day when Paxton walked into the barn.

"We're leaving in a little bit," Paxton said. "Could you do me a favor?" He looked back for some reason. Maybe he didn't want Lisa to hear what he was saying.

Quincy turned from tightening the cinch. "Depends what it is."

"Could you check on Jenny?"

"Why?" he asked warily.

"We've been friends for a long time and she was upset." Paxton twisted on his boots in the soft dirt of the barn, much like he had when he was a kid. "I just want to make sure she's okay."

"It's too late for that, Pax. You're engaged to someone else, so it's time to forget Jenny."

"I know that, but…"

"No buts. A clean break is best. Besides, Jenny is moving on. Last I heard she was dating a new intern at the hospital."

"What?" Paxton's eyebrows slammed together beneath his Stetson. "That was fast."

"Yeah. You can stop worrying about Jenny."

Quincy swung into the saddle, and he wondered if his brother was really over her. His actions indicated otherwise. "Good luck on the circuit and good luck with your engagement." He rode out of the barn with an empty feeling in his gut. He wouldn't let Paxton hurt Jenny again. Family loyalty only went so far when a heart was divided.

Phoenix, Paxton and Lisa left and drove to a rodeo in Fort Worth, Texas. Lisa wanted to watch Pax ride. From there, she would fly back to Los Angeles as she had an audition for a part in a TV show.

Paxton and Phoenix had a heavy rodeo schedule for the next couple of months and they were hoping to improve their rankings enough to attend the national finals. Paxton and Lisa would have a hard time finding time for each other, but Quincy was sure they'd find a way.

Jenny hadn't brought White Dove back and he was happy his threat had worked. The horse was hers and he wanted her to have it. Dovie would be the last thing he would ever give her.

ROUNDUP ON REBEL RANCH was in full swing. They found a bull that had a scratch behind his ear and it was swollen and looked infected.

"He must've stuck his damn head through the barbed wire," Falcon said, eyeing the red-and-white-faced bull huddled in the portable pens with the cows and calves. "It's best to herd him back to the corral at the house and use the squeeze chute. Once he gets riled up, these pens won't hold him. Quincy, Jude and Egan can do that while we finish up here."

"We're on it," Quincy said as he rode into the herd and cut the bull toward the gate. Jude and Egan were waiting, and it was a mad race to the corral.

The bull wanted to go everywhere but toward the pen. At times he'd turn and charge the horses, but the horses were expert quarter horses and easily swerved out of harm's way. Jude pulled his rope and swatted the animal's rear a couple times to keep him going straight. Dust billowed behind them as the bull picked up his speed.

John Rebel had installed a long alley to the corral for when they rounded up cattle. It was about a mile long and once they reached it, the animal would go straight into the corral, except the gate was closed. Egan rode ahead to open it. Quincy and Jude continued to dog the bull until they reached the alley. They picked up the pace and the bull loped straight toward the corral. Quincy quickly dismounted, closing the gate.

The bull ambled to the water trough and drank. Even though the heat of October wasn't bad, the bull had come a long way and was thirsty.

"Let him drink and calm down," Quincy said to his brothers.

Jude climbed the fence by the water trough

to examine the bull's head. "It looks bad. He's going to need an antibiotic shot."

"Get the supplies," Quincy ordered, so they'd have everything when they got him in the chute. They had plenty of medicine on hand from the local vet.

After a few minutes, Quincy and Egan jumped into the pen with ropes. The corral was too small to bring a horse in. The bull could do a lot of damage before the horse could get out of its way. Egan lightly swung the rope at the bull's rear and the bull yanked up his head, slinging snot and ready to fight. But when Quincy threw his rope, the bull swung around and ran into the squeeze chute. Quincy slammed the gate shut and the animal was held tight, but he still kept fighting, even shaking the chute.

Quincy stroked him. "Calm down, boy. We're just trying to help you. Calm down. It's okay."

The bull snorted and stilled for a moment.

Egan took a look at the wound. "Damn. There're maggots in there."

Jude jumped from the pipe railing. "I'll get the tweezers from the medical kit."

Quincy continued to calm the animal, and soon he stopped fighting. Jude gave him an injection in the shoulder muscle and that agitated the bull again.

"We have to get the maggots out," Egan said.

Quincy moved to the top of the chute to take a look, and he could see the little white critters. *Damn, how did this happen?* They checked the animals every day. Jude handed him a pair of big tweezers.

"What's wrong with the bull?" a voice Quincy knew all too well shouted.

He looked up to see Jenny leaning over the fence, watching them. What was she doing here?

"He has an infected scratch," Jude told her,

as if it was the most normal thing in the world for Jenny to be here.

"I'll take a look." Jenny climbed over the fence and into the corral in jeans, boots and a long-sleeved shirt, much as she always wore on the ranch. Her hair, held back in a ponytail, framed the smooth skin of her face. His pulse slid into high gear at the sight of her.

Quincy jumped to the ground, looped a rope around the bull's head and then tied it to the chute so he couldn't move his head. The bull let out a loud guttural sound. Quincy got as close as he could to the wound, all the while talking soothingly. "It's okay, boy. Just stay calm."

Jenny moved in closer, and it was doing a number on his ability to do his job. What was she doing here?

"Oh, good heavens," she said, inspecting the infected cut. "I've never seen this before. You know, maggots eat away dead flesh. Some say it's nature's cure for infected wounds, but then, that sounds absurd. We need to get the maggots out by flushing the wound."

We.

"Jenny, I'm trying to keep the animal calm here. We need to do this as fast as possible. Damn!" The bull dumped a wallop of a cow patty in the chute. The stench and the heat should gag the maggots and solve the problem. It was working on him.

Jenny, unaffected by the odor, calmly squatted by the medical kit Jude had open on the ground. "Great, a big syringe and hydrogen peroxide." She filled the syringe. "Do y'all have any four-by-fours?"

"I have a 4x4 truck," Egan quipped.

"Funny." She made a face at him. "I need something to saturate and wipe the wound."

"Here are some small rags we buy by the hundreds." Jude handed her a pack.

She pulled one from the package. "Do you have latex gloves?"

The bull grunted and tried desperately to move his head. "Jenny, we're doctoring a wound on a bull who is not in the best of moods at this moment. Could you just hurry?" Sweat trickled down his back in beads of frustration.

She stood with the syringe and towel in her hand. "You know you can catch diseases from animals and you need to be careful."

"Jenny…"

"Okay."

Quincy tightened the rope a little tighter as she flushed the wound with hydrogen peroxide. The bull jerked, but he was held firm. The maggots began to wiggle and fall on the ground. Jude stomped on them with his boots. She then used tweezers to pluck out the rest. After that, she rinsed the wound again and applied Betadine. Once they were satisfied—or rather Jenny—that the wound was clean, they backed the bull out of the chute.

That was when the animal became riled again.

Once outside the chute in the corral, he threw up his head and pawed the ground, just daring one of them to come near him.

They had a small pasture connected to the corral for sick animals that needed medical attention. "I'll open the gate," Quincy yelled, trying to stay as far away from the bull as he could. He opened it and stood behind it while Egan and Jude swung their ropes at the bull to steer him toward the opening. In a fit of temper, the bull swung round and round and then shot toward the gate. But he wasn't going without a fight. Kicking out with his back legs, he hit the gate and it knocked Quincy into the pipe railing hard. He landed with his shoulder slammed against the pipe. Pain shot up his arm and into his neck.

"Quincy!" Jenny screamed.

The world spun around and he staggered and balanced himself on the fence with his other hand.

Jude and Egan got the bull into the pasture and Quincy stumbled toward the gate.

"Are you okay?" Jenny asked, running to his side.

His shoulder ached and burned. Suddenly everything swayed and he blinked, trying to focus, trying to stand upright, trying not to show any weakness.

"Quincy!" Jenny cried a moment before Quincy crumpled to the ground.

JENNY FELL DOWN beside Quincy. He was out cold and his sun-browned skin looked so pale. Checking his breathing, she called out to Jude. "Bring those rags and some water."

Egan knelt beside her. "Is he okay?"

She checked his head and neck for bruises. Jude was back with the rags and water and Jenny didn't answer. She was too worried about Quincy. Hands shaking, she wadded several rags together and then gently tucked them beneath Quincy's neck. She soaked a rag in water, squeezed it out and wiped his face. Then she placed the cloth on his forehead.

Quincy, please wake up. Please.

He lay unresponsive.

She grabbed the front of his shirt and yanked. The snaps popped opened, revealing a broad, muscular chest. Carefully pushing it off his shoulder, she saw dark bruises along his upper arm, shoulder and his rib cage. The skin was quickly turning blue. She was usually calm in these kinds of situations, but her heart raced and her hands were clammy. *It's different when it's someone you love.*

Whoa! What? Wha...?

She didn't love Quincy. Then, why was her heart racing like a train on a fast track?

"Oh, man, he's banged up pretty bad," Egan said.

Jenny rinsed the cloth once again and wiped

the strong lines of Quincy's face, so lovable, so dear to her. "Quincy, wake up."

When he didn't stir, her breath caught in fear. "We have to get him to an emergency room."

Jude jumped to his feet. "I'll bring the truck around."

A moan erupted from Quincy's throat and Jude hurried back.

Jenny stroked back Quincy's damp hair. "Quincy."

His eyes slowly opened and relief surged through her. Glancing up at them, he muttered, "What the hell…?"

"Let's get him into the barn, out of the sun," Jenny ordered.

Egan and Jude prepared to lift their brother to his feet, but Quincy suddenly stood up on his own. Staggering a little, Quincy took several steps, and Jude and Egan were there to catch him if they needed to. Jenny hurried ahead with the cloth and water as they made their way inside the barn.

Quincy eased onto a bale of hay. "What's my shirt doing open?"

"How do you feel?" Jenny asked, taking his pulse.

He pulled his arm away. "Fine. I blacked out for a minute, that's all."

Sliding his shirt away, she said, "Look at your arm and ribs. You need to go to the emergency room. You might have fractures or even a broken bone."

"Stop fussing, it's nothing."

She placed her hands on her hips. "Okay, Quincy Rebel, this is the way it's going to go. Jude is bringing your truck and you and I are going to Temple to the emergency room. That's it. No arguments."

"I'm not going to the ER for a bruise. That's my last word."

Dealing with the bull was easier than dealing

with Quincy. It definitely had something to do with that Rebel manly pride. Men! She looked at Egan and Jude. "I need you to help me get him in the truck."

"Jenny, if I feel bad tomorrow, I'll go." Quincy made a last-minute effort, but she wasn't having any of it. He was hurt and he was going.

She pulled her phone out of her back pocket and Quincy's dark eyes watched her.

"What are you doing?"

"Calling your mother. I have a feeling she'll say otherwise."

"I make my own decisions." He frowned so deep his forehead looked like ruts.

She shrugged. "I'm a nurse and I can see you're hurt and I'm going to do everything I can to get you to a doctor. That's it. Let's go or I'm calling your mother."

"You play dirty."

"Yeah. I learned from the best."

Their eyes locked for a minute. Hers were determined. His just as determined. Grimacing, he got to his feet and snapped up his shirt. Jude and Egan followed them to the truck. With a scowl, Quincy got in. Jenny ran around to the driver's side.

"Egan, could you unsaddle my horse? I don't want her to stand out there with the saddle on while I'm gone."

"Sure thing, we'll take care of your horse. Just take care of Quincy."

Jenny backed out and off they went to Temple. Quincy leaned his head against the seat and closed his eyes.

"Try not to go to sleep. You probably have a concussion." She hated to be so bossy, but his welfare was at stake.

He sat up straight. "What are you doing at Rebel Ranch, Jenny? I thought you were starting over without any contact with the Rebels. Yet, here you are. I'm just wondering what's going on."

The tone of his voice was laced with anger and she didn't blame him. She was being pushy, but she had a reason. "I was out checking my dad's herd. We sold some cows and calves and, as you know, mama cows will look for their calves even when they weigh six hundred pounds. While I was near your property, I noticed Prairie Flower and Snowbird were fighting, or nipping at each other like horses are known to do. Since they're both pregnant, I thought you might be concerned, so I put Snowbird in her stall until you can figure out what to do. I was just leaving when y'all rode in with the bull."

"Uh…thanks…I guess. I'm not in a thanking mood right now."

"Really? No one could have ever guessed."

They arrived at the emergency room and nothing else was said. Jenny waited at the nurse's desk while they checked Quincy's shoulder and ribs. She talked to the nurse on duty and then took a chair and waited some more. Her feelings were bursting all over the place, and she was still feeling the aftereffects of her thoughts about Quincy.

They'd been friends for so long. Could friendship have turned into something more for her? Her thoughts were always on Paxton, but lately she'd been noticing a lot about Quincy. Mainly because he was always there when she needed someone. That wasn't love. That was friendship. Round and round her thoughts went, torturing her.

Her new life had just taken a detour into absurdity. Or maybe into something wonderful?

Chapter Seven

Quincy was in pain—piercing, burning hot pain. But he would never admit that, especially to Jenny. He lay on an examining table while a doctor inspected his shoulder and ribs. The smell of antiseptic, alcohol and something he couldn't describe clogged his senses. They X-rayed his shoulder and ribs and he waited, rather impatiently.

Memories of Jenny floated through his mind like bits of driftwood, jarring and disturbing. His heart knocked painfully in his chest. What was she doing back at the ranch? She'd explained, but...

The curtain opened and the object of his distress walked in. "Hey, cowboy, are you still mad?"

He swallowed to ease the dryness in his throat. His mouth tasted as if he'd been sucking on cotton. "At myself."

She smoothed his tousled hair and then laid the back of her hand against his forehead. *Don't touch me.* But the softness of her hand against his skin made all thoughts leave him. Other parts of his body were on fire now and he wanted her to leave. He didn't want her to see him like this.

She reached for his right hand and took his pulse. "Steady and strong. Good."

Yeah, that was his thought, too.

"Are you in pain?"

"No," he lied without a second thought.

Closing his eyes, he tried to relax. His arm was hurting and he just wanted Jenny to leave. He'd gotten used to being without her and he didn't want to rouse all those old feelings again. Not that they had ever left. He'd adjusted, though.

"I'm sorry you're angry," she said, and he didn't respond. "Not going to talk, huh? You take stubbornness to a new level."

He turned his head to look at her and wanted to laugh. He felt like a heel. They would always be friends and he didn't understand why he was being so testy. Then he did. He didn't want to be her friend. He wanted so much more, but loyalty to his brother and family kept him silent.

"The doctor should be in any minute. He's viewing the X-rays." Reaching through the railing, she touched his hand and everything he felt for her slammed into him like a sucker punch. He drew a deep breath and wanted to move his hand, but she entwined her fingers with his and he was lost. With her other hand she stroked his forearm and his heart galloped like a wild steed. Her touch made him crazy and he wanted to reach for her and hold her against himself, to feel her softness against his hardness. To know every inch of her and—

The doctor came in and interrupted his chaotic thoughts. "Good news, Mr. Rebel. There are no fractures or breaks. You'll just be in some pain for the next few days. Try to keep working your shoulder and not let it get stiff. From what you told us and from our exam, we don't believe you hit your head. You passed out from the pain. I'll write a prescription for some pain pills."

"I don't need any pills."

The doctor lifted an eyebrow and walked out. A few minutes later, Quincy and Jenny were on the way back to the ranch. They didn't talk much. He just wanted to get home and end this terrible day. Jenny drove to Grandpa's house and they got out and were met by a family mob.

Elias, Falcon, Egan, Jude, Grandpa and his mother were waiting. It was overwhelming.

Someone would think he was really sick the way everyone was acting.

He sat on the sofa, not saying a word. His mom sat beside him and touched his forehead with the back of her hand. Jenny had done the same thing. Jenny? Where was she?

"You need to lie down, Quincy," his mother said. "I'll bring supper over later."

"There's no need to do that," he told her. "We have plenty of food here. You've worked all day and you don't need to be waiting on me. I'll rest tonight, and tomorrow I'll be back in the saddle."

His brothers laughed and he wanted to hit them. He leaned back on the sofa and let their voices go right over his head. Was Jenny in the kitchen? Or had she left? If she'd left, that meant she was saddling her horse to ride home in the dark. He suddenly got to his feet and headed for the door.

"Quincy!" voices shouted behind him.

"I'll be back in a minute!" he told them and walked straight toward his barn.

The moonlight lit a path for him and the air held an early chill of fall. His arm ached, but he steadily made his way inside the barn and into the corral where Jenny was tightening the cinch on a saddle.

"You don't need to be riding at night. I'll take you home."

She swung around. "Oh, Quincy, you scared me." She went back to saddling the horse. "I'll be fine. I've ridden in the dark before and I need to get Sassy home." She turned to face him. "And you need to be resting."

"Don't start again."

"Okay. You're in the mood for an argument, so let's have one. You're upset because I forced you to go to the ER. Sorry, it's just the way I am. If you have something to say, just say it and then I'm going home to people who appreciate me."

Some of his anger dissipated. "I appreciate you. And thanks for helping with the bull and taking care of the problem with the mares. I'll look into it tomorrow."

She moved closer to him. The dazzling moonlight and the serenade of crickets combined with her nearness wove a hypnotic web. "Well, Quincy Rebel, is that an apology?"

"Could be..."

She touched his face with her hand, stroking it lightly. His thoughts became jumbled and he felt sure he was dreaming.

"I like you, Quincy."

"I like you, too."

"Let's stop fighting, then. Kissing is so much better." She reached up and touched his lips with hers and the night faded into a moment of pure fantasy. His fantasy. His arms encircled her waist and he drew her closer and closer, not even thinking about his arm or the pain. All he thought about was her and her touch and the moment he first kissed the woman he loved.

She wrapped her arms around his neck and his lips took hers in a kiss that rivaled the heat of a blazing fire. All of his feelings came to the surface as his lips tasted her sweetness. She opened her mouth and he deepened the kiss to a level he needed. The kiss went on and on and there was no one but the two of them in the whole universe.

Slowly, she drew away and he felt empty and lost. She swung into the saddle and rode out of the corral. He looked after her and thought that maybe she was a mirage. That he was really dreaming. But dreams were never that good.

As THE MORNING light peeped over the tall oaks, Jenny sat on the back stoop, trying to sort out her chaotic thoughts. *She loved Quincy.* How could she have missed that? And he had kissed her as if he felt the same way. Could Quincy have feelings for her, too? Her mind was ablaze with possibilities, especially after that explosive kiss. She could still feel his lips on hers—taking, yet giving everything she needed. Sweet and gentle and caring. Yet strong and masculine and evocative.

She wrapped her arms around her waist. Could there be a future for them? Probably not. Since she'd been involved with Paxton, he would never ask her out or anything like that.

But after she'd initiated the kiss, he'd kissed her back. And then some. What did that say? She was naive about affairs of the heart, but Quincy had to have feelings for her. Didn't he?

White Dove frolicked in the field with Sassy and Jenny knew she would never return the horse now. And when the thought ran through her mind she knew she had strong feelings for Quincy. How strong she wasn't sure, but she was willing to find out. There was just one little problem. Were her feelings a rebound thing or were they real? That was what scared her to death. She didn't want to hurt Quincy. She wanted to love him with all her heart, and not just because her heart was broken.

What was she going to do?

Just then, her cell buzzed. She quickly reached for it on the stoop in case it was Quincy. It wasn't. It was Paxton. She stared at the phone, wondering if she should answer. She had no desire to talk to Paxton, but she couldn't deny that spark of excitement in her chest. Old habits died hard.

"Hey, babe, how you doing?"

Jenny frowned. "Why are you calling me? The last I heard you were engaged."

"I was just worried about you. I'm sorry I hurt you."

This was the Paxton she knew. He could apologize better than any person she'd ever met. All the anger she had after hearing of his engagement seemed to have evaporated. She wasn't angry or hurt anymore.

She'd ignored or forgiven Paxton's bad behavior so many times she'd lost track. When they had an argument and he would leave for the circuit, she'd get a call just like this. "Hey, babe" as if nothing had ever happened. And she would fall right back into his arms.

But not anymore. She would not go down that road again. Her heart was full of a new kind of warmth, and she wanted to give her feelings for Quincy a chance. Paxton still had a piece of her heart, though.

"Why are you calling?"

"I wanted to tell you I scored a ninety on White Lightning in Denver. That's the best I've ever ridden."

"Did you hit your head?"

"What? Hell, no."

"Why do you think that would be something I'd want to hear?"

"Stop being angry, Jenny. You're always interested in how I score."

"I'm not angry anymore."

"You sound different."

"I am. I've finally grown up and accepted that you and I have no future. You were right."

"Jenny, I didn't mean to hurt you."

Her heart didn't even skip a beat like it had so many times when he'd apologized. "You've already told me that."

"Jenny—"

"I'm happy you scored a ninety and I hope you make it to the National Finals Rodeo. You've worked hard and you deserve it. But, please, don't call me anymore. I'm moving on, as you have."

"Okay, babe. I'll talk to you down the line."

She clicked off and stared at her phone. So easy. Yet a part of her, and she hated to admit it, was still hanging on to that young love that had gotten her through her teenage years. But it would not keep her from loving again.

The screen door opened and her dad came out. "Girl, what are you doing out here? I thought you were still sleeping."

"I was just thinking."

He came down the steps and stood there staring at her, leaning on his cane. His old worn hat was pulled low, shading his eyes. He had just turned sixty-two, but he looked much older with his white hair and stooped figure. His hair had turned completely gray two weeks after her mother had died.

"Last night you said Quincy got hurt. Are you worried about him?"

She shook her head. "He's going to be fine. A little grouchy, but fine. Paxton just called me."

"Oh, goodness, not again."

"How do you know when love is real, Dad?

How did you know your love for Mom was real?" Her dad really wasn't a talker and she had no idea why she was asking him these questions. She was just conflicted about her feelings for Quincy and Paxton, and the only way to sort them out was to talk.

He placed both hands over the top of the cane, looking off into the distance at the horses in the pasture. "When I was in high school, I met a girl who I thought was 'the one,' as you kids call it. We made plans to get married and then one day someone told me they'd seen her with someone else at a party. It turned out to be true. She was seeing two guys at the same time. That was it for me. I was off women for a long time. I was twenty-six when I met your mom. She was buying *kolaches* at the Wiznowski Bakery. She was like a magnet and I couldn't take my eyes off her. The next week, I met her at the grocery store and found out she was staying in Horseshoe with a family friend and going to nursing school in Temple. I was smitten with her and six months later we were married. Nine months later, Lindsay came along and then we were blessed with you. We didn't have a lot, but we were happy. She didn't deserve to go so early." His voice cracked on the last word.

Jenny got up and hugged him.

He wiped away an errant tear. "Or at least not before me."

She wanted that kind of love. One that would last into eternity. The problem was she wasn't completely sure how she felt about Quincy, and she didn't want to encourage a relationship because she didn't want to hurt him.

Her dad patted her shoulder. "You'll figure it out. Your heart will lead you in the right direction."

"Thanks, Dad."

"I'm going to check on the cows and, when Lindsay gets up, we'll put out some hay."

"Okay." She sat back on the stoop and made a decision. Until she knew what she wanted, she'd stay away from Quincy. He was too nice a man for her to hurt.

Chapter Eight

Quincy had a restless night. His arm and ribs ached and burned and he was forced to take a couple of Tylenol just to get some rest. Damn bull! When he pulled on his shirt, it was tight across his left shoulder, which meant his arm was swollen. But it wasn't going to keep him from working.

In the kitchen he found Elias cooking breakfast and Grandpa giving instructions. "Look who's cooking," Grandpa quipped when he saw Quincy. Elias wasn't known for his culinary skills.

"Eggs, bacon and biscuits are on the stove if

you want food," Elias said, and sat down to eat what he'd piled onto his plate.

Quincy filled a cup with coffee, feeling he was going to need a lot more to start the day.

"How are you this morning?" Grandpa asked.

"A little sore, but fine." He filled a plate and took a seat at the table.

"Jenny'll be over here to make it all better." Elias had a smirk on his face.

"What was Jenny doing here yesterday?" Grandpa wanted to know.

"Yeah, Quincy. We'd like to know."

Elias loved to pick and pick until he got a reaction, but Quincy wasn't reacting. Last night was still very vivid in his mind and he was trying to work through all his conflicting thoughts. Everything he ever wanted could come true. That frightened him because by doing so he could hurt someone he loved. Life was hell sometimes, but he wasn't backing away from his feelings for Jenny.

He got up and headed for the door without answering Elias.

"Where you going?" Grandpa called. "You're hurt and you're not supposed to work today."

Quincy kept walking.

"Why doesn't anyone ever listen to me?" Grandpa asked as Quincy closed the screen door. He wasn't in a mood to be mollycoddled.

Breathing in the fresh country air, he relaxed as he walked to the big barn. His boots left tracks in the morning dew coating the grass, and the wind fanned his face with a welcoming breath. There was no place like home.

Leaning against the pipe corral, he watched the bull, who seemed fine munching on feed in a trough. They'd take him back to the herd in a couple of days. He then let his horses out into the pasture, keeping a close eye on Prairie Flower and Snowbird. They weren't fighting with each other, so Quincy made his way to the office.

On the way his cell buzzed. He pulled it out of his pocket, wincing as a pain shot up his arm. It was Paxton. A load of guilt blindsided him.

"Hey, Quincy, I heard you had an encounter with a bull. Don't you know you're supposed to get out of their way? They're bigger than you." Evidently, his brothers had been talking, spreading the news.

"Yeah, I learned that the hard way. Just a few aches and pains that I'll get over quickly."

"Have you checked on Jenny?"

Quincy clenched his teeth until his head hurt. Why did everyone think he could solve their problems? "I saw her yesterday and she was fine."

"I talked to her, too, and she seems different. She's not mad at me anymore."

"Does that bother you?"

"No, I just don't feel good about the way I hurt her."

Quincy closed his eyes and counted to three. "How are you and Lisa?"

"She's in California and I'm in Colorado. That says it all. I don't like this long-distance relationship."

"I don't know what to tell you about that."

"Just watch out for Jenny."

He took a deep breath. "No, Pax, I'm not looking out for Jenny. She's not my responsibility. Nor is she yours. Jenny can take care of herself and it's time for you to let go."

"Yeah. Take care of yourself and I'll talk to you later."

Quincy slipped the phone into his pocket with a sigh. Last night was just a dream because it couldn't be his future. He could never hurt his brother. Even though Paxton was with Lisa at the moment, Quincy couldn't take his relationship any further with Jenny because it would cause irreparable damage within the family.

He was relegated to office duty for the day,

which he hated. But he didn't complain because his shoulder was hurting. He answered the phone, did paperwork and midday he went to check on his horses again. Everything was normal. He was about to go back to the house when Jenny walked into the barn. All his resolutions and good thoughts disappeared without a flickering doubt.

Her hair was up in a ponytail and pieces of hay were in it. He'd seen her like this many times. She and her hair had this constant battle. It was one of the small things he loved about her. She didn't care how her hair looked, but it drove her crazy when it got too bushy or hung in her face. Jenny was so wrong for him in so many ways, but his heart had a hard time adjusting to that thought.

"Hi," she said, and a moment of tension sneaked in because of last night.

"Hi, Jenny Rose," he replied, and pointed to her hair. "You have hay in…"

"Oh, crap." She shook her head, but some of the hay didn't budge. He didn't point that out.

She held up something she had in her hand. "I have an ice pack for your shoulder."

"I don't need an ice pack." He didn't mean to be defensive, but they needed to keep their distance, and defense was the only way he knew how to do that.

She glared at him, her dark eyes flashing a message he knew well. He wasn't fooling her for a minute. "How do you feel?"

"Fine. A little stiff, but fine."

"I'd like to look at your arm and ribs, please," she said. "As a nurse," she added quickly.

"Jenny…"

She lifted an eyebrow. "Less attitude would be helpful."

He didn't want to fight or argue with her so he sat down on a bale of hay and unsnapped his shirt. She sat down beside him and gently touched the bruises. Her fingers were as soft as down feathers as they stroked his skin. He remained tense, unyielding to her touch, but other parts of his body weren't so accommodating.

"Are you experiencing any pain?"

"A little." He didn't lie because he knew as a nurse she would know that he was.

"This is an ice pack and it will help the swelling and the pain. You just fill it with ice and…"

"I know the drill."

She sighed. "Quincy, I thought we'd reached an understanding last night, or are you just grouchy 'cause you're in pain?"

He took the ice pack and laid it beside him. "I got a call from Paxton this morning." He responded the only way he knew how—honestly.

She shifted uneasily. "He called me, too."

He looked into her dark eyes. "Do you see the conflict here?"

"I'm free to be with anyone I want and so are you. That's not a conflict for me. I just…"

"What?"

"I like coming here and being with you and helping with the horses, and I don't see why I have to change that because of Paxton. I'm willing to take this one day at a time if you are."

He had to make a decision and he prayed it was the right one for all of them. Paxton had moved on and Quincy didn't see any reason for him to deprive himself of something he wanted so badly. *Buts* clambered in his head like unruly children. He ignored them.

He sucked air into his tight chest. "Okay."

She smiled, and Quincy knew he'd made the right decision.

JENNY HAD HAD every intention of staying away from Quincy, but the more she thought about it, the more she wanted to be with him. She wanted to explore everything she was feeling for him even if it was wrong. She might regret it later, but for now she was taking a chance.

Quincy snapped his shirt closed and she didn't

look away from the rippling muscles of his chest and arms. Even the bruises were sexy to her. Quincy was sexy, tempting, and she might just be falling off her good-girl pedestal. But what a reward.

The next day she had to work, but as soon as she got home she changed and hurried over to Quincy's. Since it was fall, darkness fell early and as she tied her horse to the fence, the dwindling shadows disappeared into inky nothing.

The barn door was open and the light was on. Quincy came from his office looking tired and exhausted. His clothes were streaked with dirt, manure and blood. He must've just gotten in from a day on the ranch.

"Hey, Jenny Rose." He smiled a crooked smile that did a number on her senses.

"You're the only one who calls me that. I used to hate it in school, but I like the way you say it."

"How's that?"

"With affection."

The horses neighed in agitation, pushing against the corral gate wanting into the barn, and interrupting the special moment.

"My fans await," he said and walked toward the gate.

"I'll help." They worked side by side with the horses, settling them down for the night. They worked well together. They always had. In perfect harmony.

"Now for our reward." She picked up the small ice chest she'd brought into the barn and they sat and drank beer and ate peanuts. It was intimate and wonderful. Just the two of them.

"How's the arm?"

"Much better. We vaccinated, tagged and branded about seventy calves today. My arm got a workout and it's fine."

"There are a lot of cattle on Rebel Ranch."

He took a swig of Bud Light. "Yeah, and it takes all of us to keep this ranch running. But with the winter months setting in, we'll have some downtime."

"Are you through with the roundup?"

"Just about."

His cell buzzed and he pulled it out of his pocket, grimacing. "No, Grandpa, do not put anything on to cook....No, not even scrambled eggs. Just watch TV until I get there....What do you mean the TV doesn't work? Just press Power....Okay. Okay. I'll be there in a minute."

Quincy took care of his grandfather and she loved that about him. Tonight it was an inconvenience, though, but she understood. Quincy was devoted to his family. That was who he was.

He slipped the phone back into his pocket. "I better go. Elias has already left for Rowdy's. If I don't, that old man will probably burn down the house, and he's screwed up the TV once again."

She placed the cans into the ice chest and stood. On impulse, she went into his arms and leaned against him.

"Jenny, I'm filthy."

"As long as the filth is wrapped around me, I'm okay."

His arms held her tight and they stood there in the glow of the single lightbulb, just needing each other. She stood on tiptoes to kiss his lips and he returned the kiss with a fierceness she was beginning to love. He tasted of beer, peanuts and Quincy. She felt woozy just from the contact.

"I'll see you tomorrow," he whispered and headed for the side door.

She picked up the ice chest and moved toward the back door. Hot, hot, hot, that was how she was for Quincy, and all those flames were going to explode into the best night of her life. She knew that beyond a doubt. Feeling giddy, she sang "A Natural Woman" all the way home. Yes, life was looking good.

FOR THE NEXT few days they saw each other every day. The more time she spent with him the more it felt right. He made her laugh. He made her mad. And he made her happy. They had their own little world and she didn't want anyone else to intrude.

She rode over early one afternoon because she had the day off and couldn't wait to see Quincy. After putting the ice chest in the barn, she went outside. She noticed Prairie Flower in a corner by herself and Jenny went inside the corral to see what was wrong with her. Talking soothingly to her, Jenny rubbed the horse's face and she whinnied. She was a gorgeous red-and-white paint and friendlier than the others. She was a sweetie. On her rump was something Jenny couldn't make out so she grabbed Prairie Flower's halter and guided her to the water trough.

Quincy walked out of the barn at that moment and her heart beat a little faster at the sight of his tall, lean figure.

"You're early," he said, leaning on the fence.

"I'd planned to be even earlier, but Mrs. Satterwhite called. She had knee surgery two weeks ago and she's worried her incision isn't healing. It's fine. She's just lonely, I think. Then I stopped by Brianna's, a waitress from Rowdy's. Her little girl had a tonsillectomy and the girl was really scared. I took her coloring books and crayons. She's fine, too."

"Do you soothe everyone's worries?"

"You bet." She smiled at him. "Do you have any worries that need soothing?"

"You can soothe mine later," he replied with a crooked smile that created a flicker of warmth deep in her belly. "What's wrong with Prairie Flower?"

"Uh…" For a moment she lost track of the conversation. "I…I don't know. There's something on her rump I can't make out and I was going to stand on the water trough to see."

"I'll look. I'm taller than you."

"It'll only take a minute." She stepped up

onto the rim of the trough and looked at Prairie Flower's rear. "Oh, no. One of the horses has been biting her and I think we know who it is."

"Damn, I'll have to separate them now." He leaped over the fence.

"I'll bring her in for the night." Jenny reached for the halter and misjudged the space between the trough and the horse. She lost her balance and went flying backward into the water. Totally submerged, she kicked out with her feet and splashed her arms.

"It's two and a half feet of water. Stand up."

She stopped struggling, spit water out of her mouth and glared at Quincy. "You think this is funny?"

He had the audacity to grin. "Yeah."

She cupped her hands and threw water at him. He jumped back, but not before her target landed on his chest.

"Okay." He held up his hands. "Let's call a

truce." He walked to the trough and looked down at her. "Are you okay?"

She slipped and slid in the trough until she stood up. "Now you ask?"

Looping one arm around her waist, he hauled her out and strolled with her to the barn and deposited her on some loose hay. She was soaked from her head to her toes, including her boots. She smelled of horse and she should be miserable, but she found herself laughing.

Quincy laughed, too. Big hearty laughs she'd never heard from him before, and it was uplifting. He was happy and it opened up a whole new world of confidence for her.

"I'll get some towels out of my office, and I think I have an old shirt in there, too."

While she got out of her clothes, Quincy brought the horses in for the night. When he returned, she was sitting in the hay in his big shirt, feeling warm and excited in a way that rejuvenated her. Her whole body relaxed and she treasured these moments with Quincy.

"You look comfortable." He sank down beside her and removed his hat.

She touched the rattails of her hair. "And drenched. I can't believe I lost my balance." She slapped his arm. "And I can't believe you laughed."

His eyes darkened and the sound of the horses faded away. It was just the two of them alone with their feelings. She wanted to be kissed. Badly.

"I hope your grandfather is busy tonight." The words came out breathless.

"He's eating at Falcon's," he replied, his eyes, simmering with awakened passion, never leaving hers. The one lightbulb in the barn made it cozy and perfect. Even the smells of manure, alfalfa and dust were enticing.

"Good."

He picked up a towel and rubbed her hair,

then looped it around her neck and pulled her forward, his lips meeting hers in a passionate kiss. She scooted closer, wrapped her arms around his neck and pulled him down into the hay with her. This was how she wanted to be with Quincy. As close as possible. As close as lovers.

His lips trailed to the corner of her mouth, to her cheek, to the warmth of her neck, and desire, as strong as she'd ever felt, hummed through her in quest of the perfect melody that would rock her world.

The buttons on her shirt came undone easily with the touch of his fingers. Then his lips trailed down to her aching breast. Just when she thought the world would spin away, a cell phone buzzed.

Ignore it. Ignore it. But the sound was persistent.

Quincy lay back on the hay. "I think that's your phone."

"Yeah." She sat up and reached for her cell on top of the small ice chest she'd brought in.

"Hey, babe" was the most annoying sound she'd ever heard in her life. Why now?

"What is it, Paxton? Why are you calling me?"

Quincy stood up and walked away and she wanted to cry. Everything was perfect and now…

"We're on the road headed to Oklahoma and I just wanted to hear your voice."

"Well, I don't want to hear yours. Please stop calling me." She clicked off and threw her phone into the hay. *Damn!*

Quincy came back and sat on a bale, facing her.

"Quincy." She tugged her fingers through her tangled wet hair.

"We have to stop. Now."

"No…"

"Yes, before this goes any further. You and

Paxton have a connection. That's never going to change. You'll forgive him eventually, like always."

"He's engaged. Have you forgotten that?"

"Little by little he'll charm his way back into your life. Lisa is just a fling, like all the others. Maybe a little more serious, but it won't last."

"You don't think much of me, do you?"

"What do you mean?"

"You think I'm so weak that I'll continue to let Paxton treat me that way."

"It's a pattern, Jenny, and it'll never change."

She wanted to scream. She wanted to cry. But she did neither as she listened to her world crumbling around her once again. All the lovely feelings she had for Quincy were tarnished by her past. And Paxton. She should've known there was no future with Quincy. But she'd kept hoping. Now she knew that hope was in vain.

"Paxton is my brother and in his own way he

loves you, and I won't do anything to cause a rift within the family."

"I see." She pulled the shirt tighter around her and buttoned it with shaky fingers. Her skin still felt warm from his touch. Couldn't he see how much she loved him?

"It's difficult for me to go against my principles and loyalty to my family. You're Paxton's girlfriend, and to me you always will be."

She bit her lip to keep from screaming at him. If he wasn't willing to fight for her, what did they have? Nothing.

Daylight was ebbing away into dusk and the paints neighed a lonely sound that echoed through her heart. She stood on wobbly legs and gathered her wet clothes in her arms.

"Where do we go from here?" she asked in a forlorn voice.

"Nowhere," he replied. "But you're always welcome to come here. I should have never told you otherwise."

"Goodbye, Quincy." She ran from the barn, unable to say one more word. He'd broken her heart, and this time she didn't know if it could be repaired. But as she swung into the saddle and the light breeze cooled her skin, she had to admit there was a grain of truth in his thoughts. Paxton still had a part of her heart.

JENNY RAN INTO the house and straight to her bedroom. Lindsay quickly followed, taking in her appearance with a sharp eye.

"What happened to you?"

"I fell in the water trough."

"Are you okay?"

"No." Then she did something uncharacteristic. She burst into tears.

Lindsay sat down and hugged her. "What's wrong? You're over at Quincy's all the time. I don't even see you anymore. Did you hit your head or something? Are you in pain?"

"My heart is broken." She hiccupped.

"Oh, well, then. I'll get the Band-Aids."

Jenny wiped away tears with the back of her hands. "This isn't funny. I love Quincy, but he's not going to give us a chance."

"Why?"

"Paxton."

"Oh."

Jenny got herself under control. "It's me, too. I hate to admit this, but a part of me is still clinging to Paxton. When he calls, I get this excitement in my chest like I did when I was sixteen and he'd call and say he'd be here in five minutes. I'd rush to my room, comb my hair and put on lipstick. I can't get rid of that feeling. Why can't I, Lindsay?"

"Only you can answer that."

Jenny brushed hair from her face. "I love Quincy and I want to spend all my time with him. I can't wait to get off work to rush over there and be with him. He's strong, yet soft and gentle and he makes me feel special and loved and he's everything I've ever wanted in a man."

"You're talking in circles. You said Quincy wouldn't give your love a chance, but maybe it's you who's not?"

"Paxton called while I was there and I could just feel Quincy shutting down. His loyalty to his brother reared its damn head and he said it was over. We had to stop seeing each other."

"That's probably a good idea considering the way you're feeling. Take some time and see which feelings are the strongest. Those lingering tidbits from the past, or those that you have for Quincy. Time will give you your answer."

"I suppose." Jenny took a long breath and knew she had to get her life sorted out. She'd jumped into the relationship with Quincy too quickly. She needed time to herself and to make the right decisions for her future. Right now her heart was breaking. But tomorrow she would start over. *Again.*

ON FRIDAY AFTERNOON, Quincy made sure someone would be home to check on Grandpa, and then he headed for Plano to see Wendy. It was what he needed to clear his head of thoughts of Jenny.

Wendy lived outside of town on about ten acres in a white frame house with a garden and a small barn for a horse. Chickens pecked in the yard and a yellow lab lay on the front porch. At the sight of Quincy's truck, the lab stood and barked. The front door opened and Wendy came out with a five-year-old boy in her arms.

Wendy set the boy on his feet and he tottered down the steps and to Quincy. Little Will had been born with spina bifida and held a special place in Quincy's heart. The last time Quincy had seen the boy he had used crutches or a walker. The boy practically ran on his toes with his arms flapping until he reached Quincy.

"I'm walking, Cee." Little Will had never been able to say *Quincy* so he called him Cee.

Quincy squatted. "I'm so proud of you." Wendy worked tirelessly with Little Will's exercise program and her efforts were showing results.

"Me, too."

Quincy picked up the boy and carried him inside the house. He sat on the well-worn tweed sofa with the boy on his lap. "Have you heard from Will?"

Wendy took the recliner across from him. "Yes. We spoke on Skype last night." A petite woman with soft brown hair, Wendy had a heart of gold.

"Daddy's coming home," Little Will said.

Quincy looked at Wendy. "Is that true?"

"Yes. He's coming home for two weeks at Christmas and then in three months he'll be coming home for good. Little Will can hardly wait and neither can I."

Quincy had served in Afghanistan with Wendy's son, Will, and they had remained friends over the years. Will had chosen to re-enlist and six years ago he'd met a girl and had gotten married. Little Will had been born soon after with a birth defect, and the girl couldn't handle the stress of a child with medical problems, and they'd soon divorced. Will had full custody of his son. With Wendy's help, he was raising his boy, and Quincy knew it hurt him to be away so much. He had asked Quincy to watch out for them, so he visited as often as he could and repaired the things around the house that Wendy couldn't. Mainly, he cared for Little Will so she could get a break. But these days the boy was becoming very independent.

"Horsey." Little Will poked Quincy in the chest. Quincy had bought the boy a gentle mare and every time Quincy visited, he wanted to ride.

Later, Wendy got dressed to go to dinner and a movie with a friend. She had a sister who helped her out now and then, but other than that she had the sole responsibility of caring for Little Will. She needed some time for herself, so Quincy made sure she got some when he was there.

After she left, Quincy put a saddle on Horsey. When he was three, Will had named her. The boy helped him with the cinch. They encouraged him to do as many things as he could and he didn't like it when someone helped him unless he asked. Quincy lifted the boy into the saddle and walked Horsey around the small corral. Will's little face beamed.

Quincy had always wanted children, but that wasn't going to happen anytime soon. Without Jenny… He couldn't stop thinking about her. He just wished he could stop remembering her touch, her kiss, her smile and the way she made him feel. Maybe soon…

The next morning Wendy went into town to buy groceries and shop and Quincy took care of Will. He left about four Saturday afternoon to go to a horse auction outside Austin the next morning. After checking into a hotel, he called Grandpa to let him know he wasn't coming home just yet because he knew Grandpa would keep calling if he didn't. Nothing suited him at the auction, so he headed home early. He would make it there by noon.

It was good to get away and it was good to come home. Now he could deal with his broken heart. He didn't even look as he passed the Walker place. If he saw her…

Grandpa was sitting on the front porch with Mutt at his feet. "Hey, boy, it's about time you came home," he said as Quincy walked up the steps. Grandpa followed him into the house. Elias was lazing on the sofa in front of the TV.

"Hey, Quincy, how you doing?"

"Not as good as you."

"I fed cows all morning and I deserve some downtime on Sunday. So don't bother me."

Yep, it was good to be home and back to normal.

"Jenny came over yesterday." Grandpa stomped into the kitchen.

Unable to stop himself, Quincy swung around, his heart pounding at the sound of her name. How he hated that.

"What did she want?"

Grandpa shrugged.

"What did she say?"

"Well, let's see." Grandpa rubbed his scraggly jaw. "She said, 'Hi, Mr. Abe, is Quincy home?' I said no. She then asked if you were coming back and I told her I didn't know, that you went to see your woman friend in Plano. Her face kind of went all sad."

"Yeah, Quincy," Elias shouted from the living room. "Her face was real sad."

His gut tightened, but he didn't respond.

Grandpa kept talking. "She said she'd lost her phone and she thought it was in the barn, but the door was locked. Elias showed up and told her he'd go open the door. He started flirting and she told him to give it a rest. But she went with him and she found her phone."

"I think she has a crush on me," Elias said. "I'll have to ask her out."

"He's nuts," Grandpa said.

Quincy marched into the living room. "Stay away from Jenny."

Elias sat up. "Paxton's out of the picture. Why not?" He stood with a glint in his eyes. "Why not, Quincy?"

"I don't have to tell you why. I'm just telling you to stay away from her." Elias was goading him and Quincy wasn't going to react. Letting out a long breath, he realized he was doing just that. Reacting.

Elias eyed him with that stupid look. "For the first time in your life you want something, and if you don't go after it, then you're a fool. That's all I'm going to say."

"Good."

Elias was right. Quincy knew what he wanted, but it went against everything his father had ever taught him. It went against his principles to break the brothers' code. If there was any hope for him, though, he'd have to make a decision soon about his future.

"Your mom's waiting on us for lunch," Grandpa reminded them. "When you two get through staring at each other, we can go."

Not another word was said as they walked to their mom's house. Quincy was fine with that. He wasn't in the mood to talk. By the time they got there, everyone had arrived: Rachel and Egan. Falcon, Leah and their family. And Jericho. Of course, Jude and Zane lived there.

Rachel was holding Falcon's youngest, baby John. She kissed his head. "He smells so good it makes my ovaries kick in." She handed him to Egan. "Hold him."

"Rachel…"

Rachel placed the baby in Egan's arms and Egan was startled for a moment. He looked awkward with a child in his arms. Baby John looked around for his mother, his bottom lip trembling.

Leah immediately went to him. "Mommy's here." She took the baby and he rested his head on her shoulder. Leah held him close. Kissing his cheek, she said, "This was worth all the pain and all the suffering." Eden went to her mother.

Falcon watched his wife and children with a look of total love on his face. His brother and his family were finally happy and Quincy was happy for them, too. As he watched them, he knew he was witnessing true love. But he had a feeling that would never happen for him. His heart had taken a wrong turn somewhere and he was lost and couldn't find his way back to a future he wanted.

Chapter Nine

Jenny curled up on the sofa, exhausted from working the weekend, which she didn't normally do. But she'd needed to stay busy and the hospital had needed the extra help.

The door opened and Lindsay came in with a bag of groceries. She did the grocery shopping because she said it was relaxing after a stressful day at work. That was fine with Jenny, who'd rather be outside. Her sister gave her one of those looks and Jenny couldn't blame her. Lately, Jenny had been as conflicted as a teenager. She was supposed to be way past that. It was time to get her act together. She followed her sister into the kitchen.

Lindsay put milk and juice into the refrigerator. "What has you so sad looking, or do I even need to ask?"

"No. I'm just tired and I plan to stay that way for a long time."

Lindsay placed bread and a bag of cookies on the counter. "Just live, Jenny. Everything will work its way out. The nurses are having a party next weekend and you're going."

"I've already made plans with Beth and Jasmine. I'm looking forward to getting out and having fun."

Having fun without Quincy. Her heart ached at the thought. *Quincy.* Just thinking his name made her sad. Her head was beginning to throb, so she got up and headed for the back door.

"Where are you going?"

"To check on the horses. Don't wait on me for supper."

"Jenny…"

She closed the door and ran for the barn.

After she fed the horses, she spent time with White Dove. With a horse brush, she made long strokes down the horse's back.

When would the pain stop?

QUINCY STAYED BUSY. If he wasn't working on the ranch, he was taking care of his horses. One afternoon, he and Zane mucked out the stalls and then hauled the manure and old hay to his mom's garden to be tilled early next year. Then Zane wanted to ride the paints.

Quincy now had five mares and a two-year-old colt, the first from Red Hawk. The seventeen-hand stud was a registered Tobiano paint horse, but the mares he picked up at horse auctions across the state. Later, he would invest in some registered mares. For now, he was happy learning the breed.

He favored the Tobiano paint because of their white legs and solid face with a star or a blaze. Also, the spotted round marking pattern of more white than dark was attractive. The mares were mixed breeds and their patterns varied from speckled to bold markings.

Running Bear, the colt, was a chestnut-red-and-white paint and the horse was fast. Zane had fallen in love with the foal and Quincy had given him the horse. He'd given both his nephew and niece a horse and they helped him whenever he needed it. He was close to both of them.

Zane came through the big barn doors that led into the corral. He'd finished exercising the mares and Running Bear. Quincy had given all the horses Indian-type names: White Dove, Breaking Dawn, Snowbird, Prairie Flower, Foxy Lady and Dancing Cloud, who belonged to Eden.

Zane handed him several bridles he'd been using. "I was thinking I'd like to ride Running Bear in the Horseshoe race in the spring. He's really fast, Uncle Quincy."

Quincy hung a bridle on the wall. "Did you ask your dad about it?"

Zane shook his head. "He'll just say no. He won't let me do anything unless it has something to do with school and my studies."

There was no missing the resentment in Zane's voice, which was so unlike him. He and Jude had a good relationship, so Quincy wondered what was going on.

"What's this really about? You and your dad get along so well."

"But he won't let me do anything I want to do. It's always about how smart I am and how I need to think about college and all that kind of stuff. I'm twelve and I just want to have fun." Zane looked up at him. "Can you talk to him, Uncle Quincy, please?"

So much hope in the boy's eyes, as if Uncle Quincy could fix everything. Uncle Quincy couldn't even fix his own life, but he would never let his nephew down.

He placed an arm around Zane's shoulder. "What would you like for me to say to him?"

"Ask him if I can race Bear. The McCrays always win and I know Bear is faster than any horse they have."

"That would mean a lot to you to beat the Mc-Crays?"

"Dudley's always bragging about his horses at school. He calls me names and I want to show him that I'm a cowboy just like he is."

"What does he call you?"

"Nerd, geek, egghead, bookworm, anything to get at me. I just ignore him."

The sad voice got to Quincy. "I'll talk to your dad."

Zane's eyes lit up. "Thanks, Uncle Quincy."

"I'm not promising anything. Your dad has the last word."

"I know." Zane kicked at the dirt with the tip of his boot.

There was silence in the barn, and Zane kept staring at the dirt. "Can I ask you a question?"

"Sure."

Zane raised his head. "Do you think my mother will ever come back?"

That was a powerful question—one that Zane had never asked before. Paige had given up her baby, and Quincy wasn't sure how to ease the boy's bruised heart.

Quincy hugged Zane's thin shoulders. "I don't know, partner, and that's the honest truth. Teenagers make crazy mistakes and your mother made a big one."

"I don't want her to come back. It's not like Eden's mom. Mine gave me away because she didn't want me."

Quincy never realized how much this bothered Zane. It probably stemmed from Eden's mom returning home last year.

He squatted in front of the boy. "But there're

a whole lot of people here who want you, and love you and I'm one of them."

Zane threw his arms around Quincy's neck and hugged him. The skinny arms held on fiercely. "I love you, Uncle Quincy."

Quincy hugged him back. "Love you, too, partner."

The boy drew back. "I better go. Grandma probably has supper ready." Zane ran out of the barn and Quincy went back to his lonely, lonely life.

He missed Jenny.

Chapter Ten

Quincy hadn't heard from Jenny and that was just as well. He believed everything he'd told her. Paxton would come home soon and he and Jenny would get back together, like always. He'd been told since he was a boy that a Rebel man only loved once and he would not stand in the way of Paxton's happiness or Jenny's. He would find his footing and love a woman deeply one day. She just wasn't going to be Jenny.

He used the tractor to put a roll of hay in the pen with the horses. Since it was November, the weather was getting chilly and he usually fed them more.

As he drove the tractor into the barn, Jude walked up. His brother hesitated and then asked, "Could I talk to you for a minute?"

"What's up?"

Quincy jumped off the tractor and Jude sank onto a bale of hay. His face was creased into a worried frown, but then that was a perpetual look for Jude. For once, Quincy would like to see his brother happy.

"It's Zane. He's starting to talk back to me, and he's never done that before."

Quincy had been meaning to speak to Jude, but they always seemed to be going in different directions. Now was the perfect time. He sat by his brother and thought he really needed to get chairs for the barn. A lot of talk went on there.

"Did something happen?"

"His teacher thought it would be a good idea if Zane tutored some of the students who are having trouble with math. It would help him to not be so bored if he was helping others.

I thought it was a great idea, but he had a fit when I told him."

"You didn't discuss it first?"

"What?" Jude stared at him with dark, troubled eyes.

"You didn't ask how he felt about it?"

Jude stood and stretched his shoulders with a deep sigh. "No. I made the decision all on my own."

"Why are you treating him as if he's five years old?"

"You don't understand how hard it is to be a parent and trying to make all the right decisions when you feel as if you're making all the wrong ones."

"I know it's been difficult, but Zane is a good kid. You've done a great job with him. Don't screw it up now."

Jude resumed his seat. "Zane is different, Quincy. He's smart and he can do anything he wants if he would just apply himself."

"But what if he's not happy? Don't you want him to be happy?"

"Quincy…"

"Okay, I'm not a parent, so I don't know those deep feelings you have inside. But I know Zane. He's your son and he's just like you. He likes horses and he likes to rope and he likes to race and he loves this ranch. Going off to a big college is not on his dashboard of things to do right now. Just talk to him. Zane will listen, but stop pushing. You're pushing too hard, Jude. Let him be a little boy and enjoy this ranch like you did when you were a kid. Everything else will fall into place."

"I'm just so afraid."

"Of what?"

"Of making wrong decisions for him."

"Jude, just talk to Zane about the tutoring. Let him decide whether to continue or not. Just don't force him. And I'll tell you something just between brothers."

"Okay."

"Zane wants to ride Bear in the Horseshoe race in the spring."

Jude frowned. "What? He never mentioned that to me."

"Because he knows you'll say no without even thinking about it."

"Do I do that?"

"Yes. You don't give Zane a choice in anything."

"Do you think he can win?"

"Bear is fast and by spring he'll be really fast. The McCray boys always win and this time Zane wants to prove to them that he's a cowboy just like them."

"He tells you all this stuff?"

"He just needs to talk to someone because his dad is always thinking of his future instead of his present."

Jude stood. "I'm going to the house and have a long talk with my son."

"Just listen to his point of view."

Jude walked out of the barn and Quincy felt a pull on his heart for his younger brother. He'd had it rough raising a son on his own. But they'd all been here for him. That still wasn't the same thing, though.

The horses pushing against the gate to get into the barn snagged Quincy's attention. "I'm coming."

After getting the horses settled into their stalls for the night, Quincy went to the house to fix supper for Grandpa. He didn't feel like cooking so he just made sandwiches. Grandpa wasn't pleased.

"I wanted soup," Grandpa announced.

"I didn't have time to fix anything, but I'll do it tomorrow."

"It's gonna get colder, you know."

"Yeah." Quincy had been listening to the weather, and a cold front was coming in earlier than expected.

Elias came in, stomped the dirt off his boots on the mat and sailed his hat for the rack. "Damn, it's getting cold out there, but we got everything fed and in good shape." His brother grabbed a box of Oreos out of the pantry.

Grandpa shook his head and headed for his recliner.

"Is that all you're going to eat?" Quincy asked.

"Nah. I'm going down to Rowdy's later." Elias stuffed his face with an Oreo and then swallowed. "So?"

"I thought I might go out for a while." Quincy glanced toward his grandpa in his recliner in front of the television. He wasn't sure where he was going, but he needed to get out. It was time to start living instead of working all the time.

"Come on, Quincy. There's nothing wrong with Grandpa except a little senility. He doesn't take any medication or need watching every second of the day. You baby him too much."

"I guess."

"I know. So go out and do whatever you want to. I am. Tammy Jo's in town for a couple of days and I'm looking forward to a fun time."

"Bob's gonna kill you when he finds out you're sleeping with his daughter."

"Bob's too busy running Rowdy's to keep track of his grown-up daughter. She does have a mind of her own, you know."

Quincy shrugged. Trying to talk to Elias was like talking to a two-year-old—only so much got through. He walked into the living room. Grandpa was flipping through the channels with a deep frown. He handed Quincy the control.

"Find a good Western."

With a long sigh, Quincy did just that and settled in for the evening. The good-guy thing was going to kill him.

JENNY WAS OFF for the next three days and she hated it, but she'd worked so much overtime that Lindsay said she now had to take a break.

Since the weather was getting colder, she would stay home for her dad. Usually the cold temperatures made his leg ache and she didn't want him doing any of the heavy work on the ranch.

But she still had time to think and she finally had to admit that Quincy wasn't the cause of her heartache. She was. Her lingering feelings for Paxton were tearing her up. She wished she could take a sledgehammer and eradicate everything she'd ever felt for him. It wasn't that simple, though. Until she found a way to let go she couldn't go forward, and that drove her crazy.

She'd latched on to Quincy to keep from drowning in all her pain and he didn't deserve that. Stepping back and looking at her life was as brutal as standing in a hurricane, because it tore away her protective veneer and revealed all her faults. Her fear of being alone. Her fear of not being loved. Now she had to pick up the pieces and go forward.

It didn't keep her from thinking about Quincy.

When she'd lost her phone, she'd gone over to his house and his grandfather had told her he'd gone to see a woman in Plano. That stung. She'd forgotten about the mystery woman Quincy always visited. Whoever she was, Jenny hoped she made Quincy happy. Because, above all else, he deserved that.

She glanced out the kitchen window to see the wind whipping through the branches of the tall oaks and dark clouds gathering on the horizon. A cold front was moving through and she hoped her dad would come into the house soon. She didn't like him being out there in it, but she wouldn't tell him that. He was very touchy when she or Lindsay asked him about his leg.

Her cell buzzed and she reached for it on the counter. She saw the caller's name and took a moment before she clicked on. *Paxton*. She waited for the excitement to fill her chest, but it wasn't there. All she felt was the sadness of losing Quincy. She clicked on without a second thought.

"Hey, babe." Paxton's voice soon came through loud and clear. And annoying.

"Please don't call me babe. I hate it and I've hated it for years. I would appreciate it if you would never use it again in reference to me."

"Okay, ba— Okay. I just wanted to tell you Phoenix and I qualified to go to Vegas. We'll both be bull riding. We're excited."

So many years she waited for these calls to see how he was doing on the circuit, to see if his scores were high enough to get him to the big stage in Vegas. And the big money. Today it didn't matter. She didn't care anymore. It was a revelation. No longer was she waiting for Paxton.

"Congratulations, and tell Phoenix congratulations, too. But, please, don't call me anymore. We are really over and your career is not a top priority of mine any longer."

"C'mon, babe."

She heard the front door open and soon Lindsay walked in with a bag of groceries.

"Really, Paxton, that doesn't work on me. Please stop calling. It really is over." Saying that, she laid her phone on the table.

It really was over. For Jenny. For the first time she felt it in her heart.

"You're talking to Paxton?" Lindsay asked as she laid a package of hamburger meat on the counter.

"He keeps calling."

"Don't answer."

It is really over, and all I feel is relief.

"Jenny, are you listening to me?"

She stood with a smile on her face. "I didn't feel the excitement, Lins. It wasn't there. I'm over him. All the times he hurt me and now I can finally say I'm truly over Paxton."

Lindsay leaned against the counter. "Wow. Does that mean…?"

"No. It doesn't mean I'm running to Quincy. We both need time."

"That sounds very grown-up."

"How about that? Your little sister has finally grown up at the age of thirty-one. A little past due, but still an accomplishment."

"Good for you." Lindsay looked around the kitchen. "Where's Dad?"

"He went to look for a calf and he hasn't come back. I'm getting worried." She went to the kitchen window again and saw the headlights and she relaxed. "He's driving up now."

After supper, Jenny took a shower and tried to watch TV. She had one in her room, as did Lindsay. Their dad had complete control over the one in the living room. Nothing held her interest so she got up and went to the window. From there, she could see Quincy's barn and the light was still on. He was probably getting his paints in out of the cold.

She missed going over there. She missed

Quincy. But she couldn't lean on him any-more. To ease her heartache she had traded one brother for the other. That was like switching horses in the middle of the race. Her bad. And her new heartache.

To put it all behind her she was looking for-ward to the party on Saturday night. It was what she needed to gain a new perspective on her life.

ON SUNDAY MORNING Quincy woke up to pour-ing rain. He got dressed, made coffee and flipped on the TV to The Weather Channel. The temperature was supposed to drop throughout the day and tonight it should be almost freezing. Looked as if winter was coming early to Texas.

Grandpa trudged in, fully dressed, wearing a coat.

"Why are you wearing a coat in the house?"

"Because it's cold."

Quincy went to the thermostat and turned

up the heat and then fixed his grandpa a cup of coffee.

"You're a good grandson," Grandpa said, sitting at the table sipping his coffee. "You know that other grandson didn't come home again last night."

Quincy hadn't expected Elias after what he'd said the other day. But boys who stayed out all night bothered Grandpa. "He'll be home soon."

Elias came through the back door, shivering. Removing his slicker and hooking it on the coatrack, he said, "Damn. It's raining."

"Boy, where have you been?"

"Living." Elias poured a cup of coffee.

"You do too much *living.*"

Elias straddled a chair. "Now, Grandpa, you're always telling us to find a woman. I'm just doing research. And, Quincy." Elias turned his attention to him. "You'll never guess who I saw last night."

Quincy leaned against the counter, sipping coffee. "I'm not playing a guessing game with you."

"Aw, shucks, I was looking forward to the fun. But I'll tell you anyway because I'm that kind of guy. Tammy Jo said she wanted to go someplace nice. The moment she said that I knew she had a place already picked out, and it was an upscale nightclub packed with nurses having the time of their lives. Right there in the middle of them was Jenny. I didn't recognize her at first. She had on this short black dress, high heels and her hair was all bushy the way women wear it, all sexy and all. She was hot and downing Jell-O shots with the best of them. Interns crashed their little party and the fun was on."

Grandpa leaned over and whispered to Elias, "Are you crazy?"

"Let him talk, Grandpa. He's obviously enjoying this."

"Well, Quincy, Jenny's a completely different person when she's had a few drinks." Elias kept on as if Quincy hadn't spoken. "I danced with her. The lights were low and our bodies were moving as one, and, oh, man, she smelled good. You know what she said, Quincy?"

Quincy just stared at his brother, refusing to be goaded.

"Right there in my fantasy she said, 'How's Quincy?' I told her he was grouchy as hell and needed a nurse. She laughed and Tammy Jo put a stop to our little conversation."

Quincy kept his emotions under control. Jenny was free to go and do whatever she wanted. It had nothing to do with him. But the pain bubbling through his system belied everything he was thinking.

Grandpa broke the tension in the room. "Did I tell y'all about the time I met this widow lady who had a lot of money and was looking for a little fun?"

Quincy headed for the door. "With this weather, I'm going over to see what Falcon has planned for the day. Even though it's Sunday, we'll have to make sure all the wells have lights on them so they won't freeze up. I'll catch y'all later."

"What about breakfast?" Grandpa asked.

"Elias will fix it," Quincy replied at the door.

"Quincy—"

That was Elias's payback for his smart mouth. Quincy knew what his brother was doing and he couldn't fault him for trying to make Quincy see sense. Elias just didn't understand how hard it was.

Falcon's truck was at their mother's, so Quincy drove there. Falcon and their mom were having breakfast and Quincy joined them to talk over the day's chores.

Jude and Zane came into the kitchen. Zane grabbed a biscuit and stuffed it with scrambled eggs and bacon. Quincy noticed right off that something was different. Jude's face wasn't so pinched and Zane was smiling.

"Hey, Uncle Quincy." Zane came over to him, his words muffled as he munched on the biscuit.

"Don't talk with your mouth full," Jude told his son.

Their mother handed Zane a glass of milk and he downed it quickly, eager to talk.

"Dad and I talked last night and he said I could ride Bear in the horserace next year." Zane's eyes sparkled as if he had firecrackers going off behind them. "That's good, huh? And I told Dad I would still do the tutoring. It's not so bad and it's only twice a week and Dad said I can help on the ranch, too." Zane hugged Quincy. "Thank you," he whispered for Quincy's ears only.

How Quincy wished he could solve his own life problems that easily, but he was afraid there was no solution for his heartache. Only time could dull the pain.

And he had lots of time.

Chapter Eleven

"Quincy!" his mother called before he could get out the door. "I'm fixing homemade chicken-noodle soup for supper and I'm making enough for you, Abe and Elias. And, of course, Jericho. You can pick it up anytime after six."

"Thanks, Mom. Grandpa was asking for soup the other night. He'll be happy."

A melancholy expression came over her face. "Your dad always liked to have soup when the first cold spell came. It became a tradition and I guess I still think about that when it gets cold. I think about him."

An invisible balled fist pressed into his chest,

forcing him to take a deep breath. It was always painful when his mom talked about their dad in that sad tone of voice. He walked over and hugged her, knowing words wouldn't ease her pain or his. That was the way it was, and every now and then it was like a paid-on-account in this thing they called life.

He kissed her cheek and made his way toward the door. The day was busy and the morning faded from his mind like it always did, but the memories lingered as a reminder that part of his life was missing.

He changed lightbulbs in the heat lamps in all the well houses. His brothers were busy making sure all the farm equipment and trucks had antifreeze in them. Any busted pipes or radiators would cause them extra work and expense. After that, they rode out to check the herds to make sure there was plenty of hay in all the pastures. Grandpa even joined them, huddled in his winter coat. By midafternoon the wind shifted from the north and the temperature dropped drastically. The heavy, dark clouds hung low and the smell of rain was in the air again. He made sure Grandpa got home safely and then he went to check on the paints. He'd pick up the soup on his way back.

The horses pranced around, eager to get into their stalls for the night. Thunder rumbled across the sky and Quincy reached for his slicker and slipped into it. He already had a plastic cover over his hat. He closed the big double doors, and the cold north wind whipped around him, biting into his hands and face. He buttoned the slicker over his sheepskin coat and turned toward his truck. As he did, something in his peripheral vision caught his attention. At the same time the sky opened up with torrential rain. He squinted through the downpour and the darkness and saw lights in the pasture of the Walker place.

Were those truck lights? What was Clyde

doing out in this weather? He pulled his phone from his pocket to call Jenny, but with the rain and the weather there was no signal. The lights stayed in one place and they weren't moving. Without thinking, he leaped over the fence to see what was wrong, for he felt sure something was. He didn't take his truck because that was a good way to get stuck in the mud.

He kept hoping the rain would let up, but it continued in a steady onslaught. When he reached the spot, he saw there were two trucks. Clyde's and Jenny's. There didn't seem to be anyone around until he heard a moan. He held his hand over his eyes and tried to see more closely. Two figures were on the ground some distance away. Clyde lay lifeless and Jenny was trying to pull his body toward the truck. He fell down beside her.

"What happened?" he shouted above the rain.

Jenny took a deep breath. She was soaked from head to toe in nothing but jeans and a shirt. "He didn't come home for supper so I came looking for him and found him on the ground. I…I don't know if he's had a heart attack or a stroke and… I…I can't get him to the truck. I have to get him to a hospital." She was shouting, too, as the rain continued its assault. "Daddy, Daddy," she called, stroking Clyde's face.

Quincy reached down and gathered the limp man into his arms. "Open the back door of the truck." Jenny ran to do his bidding, sloshing through the rain.

It was difficult but Quincy managed to get Clyde into the backseat. Jenny climbed in beside him and Quincy ran around to the driver's side. He pulled off his slicker and coat and handed them to Jenny. "Maybe this will help to keep him warm."

Jenny was busy checking his vitals. "He barely has a pulse. Hurry, Quincy. Oh, no, there's blood on his clothes. And a knot on his head. He must've hit his head on something. Hurry!"

He turned the key in the ignition. "Pray we don't get stuck."

The truck slid a few times, but they made it to the gate, which was closed. He jumped out and opened it and Jenny drove through. By the time he slid into the driver's seat again, she was already in the backseat wiping water from her dad's face with a loving hand.

"I have to call Lindsay. She had to go in to the hospital. Do you have your phone? I don't know where mine is."

"It's in the pocket of my slicker, but I couldn't get a signal a little earlier."

It didn't take Jenny long to find it. "It's ringing, but she's not answering. Damn it!"

"She's probably busy." Quincy was whipping in and out of traffic, hoping a policeman or highway patrolman didn't catch him, but he knew Clyde was in grave danger.

"He's so wet and shivering. Daddy, I'm sorry I didn't come looking for you earlier." Her voice cracked and Quincy knew she was crying. His heart contracted.

"Wrap the coat around him and pull the slicker over him. Maybe it will generate some warmth," he told her.

"I think that helped," she said. "I'm going to try Lindsay again."

Lindsay answered and Jenny screamed into the phone, "Why didn't you answer the first time?" There was a slight pause as he was sure Lindsay was attempting to answer the question, and then Jenny said in a sad voice, "Daddy's had an accident. It's bad, Lindsay. I…" Jenny sobbed into the phone and Quincy reached back and took the phone from her.

"This is Quincy. We're about ten minutes away from the emergency room. Your father must've fallen and hit his head and he's unconscious, but he's alive, wet and cold. Jenny's just a little upset."

"I was in a meeting and couldn't answer the phone."

"There was nothing you could do since we were already on the road. I'm sure Jenny would appreciate it if you were there when we arrived."

"Yes, yes. I'll alert the ER."

"Thanks." He clicked off and handed the phone back to Jenny. "Take a deep breath. Your dad needs you to be calm."

"I know. I'm just so scared."

"I'm right here."

"Thank you, Quincy."

"No problem."

As he turned into the hospital parking lot, the rain let up. Driving up to the ER, he saw two orderlies with a stretcher and Lindsay standing behind them. When the truck came to a stop, Lindsay yanked open the back door.

One look at her father and Jenny, she paled

and almost crumpled to the pavement, but she held on to the door. "Oh, oh, oh, is he…is he alive?" Right before his eyes he witnessed an experienced trained nurse fall to pieces.

He hopped out and pulled Lindsay and Jenny from the vehicle. They wrapped their arms around each other, tears running down their faces. He waved for the orderlies to come forward. In minutes, they had Clyde out of the vehicle and on the stretcher and raced him into the hospital. Lindsay and Jenny ran behind the stretcher. Quincy exhaled a long breath and got back in the truck to park it in a lot. Then he ran for the entrance of the hospital, wanting to be there for Jenny. And Lindsay, too.

He found Jenny in the hallway with her arms wrapped around her waist, shivering. When she saw him, she ran into his arms and he held her as if it was the most natural thing in the world. They were wet from head to toe and they melded together in the mushy steam that emanated from their bodies.

He stroked her wet hair. "Where's Lindsay?"

"She went with Dad. They tried to stop her, but she's director of nursing so they gave up. I'm so scared, Quincy."

He looked into her sad eyes. "He's alive. Cling to that."

"I can't lose my dad. I just can't." Her words were wrapped around a sob and he held her again, trying to ease her distress.

Lindsay came through the double doors to the ER and her face was pale. Jenny ran to her. "How is he?"

"His pulse is low, as is his body temperature. He has hypothermia and they're trying to warm him up to his core temperature. He has a bump on his head and he's lost some blood, plus he has a concussion. They're taking him to the intensive-care unit where they'll do some extensive testing. He's...he's in critical condition. How long was he out in this weather?" The question was directed at Jenny, and Quincy didn't like the tone, but he stayed out of it.

"He wanted to go check on that calf he's been looking for for the past two days. I told him it was getting late and I would do it first thing in the morning. He wouldn't listen to me and I told him if he wasn't back in thirty minutes I was coming to look for him. Then he got mad and told me I treat him like a little kid and that he could take care of himself. When he didn't come back, I gave him an extra five minutes and then got in my truck and went to find him. I drove all over and that's when I really got worried. Then I saw his truck over near Quincy's barn, but he wasn't in it. I searched and searched until I saw him on the ground. I couldn't wake him and I tried to drag him to the truck so I could get him in it, but then it started to rain and I covered his body with mine. I didn't want to leave him, but I knew I had to do something.

I was going to drive to the house to call 9-1-1 when Quincy showed up."

"You should never have let him go out of the house in the first place in this weather."

Jenny stiffened. "Don't talk to me as if I'm one of your employees. He's my dad and you think I wanted him out there in this weather? Do you think I wanted him to get hurt?"

"I'm sorry," Lindsay immediately apologized. "I'm just so worried."

"Me, too."

The sisters embraced and Quincy thought only brothers fought and argued, but he guessed sisters did, too.

Lindsay drew back, eyeing Jenny's bedraggled wet and muddy appearance. "I'll send someone to get you some scrubs."

"I can get them myself," Jenny snapped.

Lindsay looked at her sister. "Let's stop arguing. I'm going to ICU while you get changed." She walked off down the hall.

Jenny turned to Quincy. "Sorry for the sister drama."

He shrugged. "I'm used to brother drama, and trust me it's much more volatile."

"I don't know what I would've done if you hadn't showed up. Oh, Quincy." She went into his arms and rested against his chest.

All his wet and tired muscles came to life. All she had to do was touch him and he felt alive and young and all male. For years, he'd denied what he felt for her, but today, here in this hallway, all those feelings were right there and he knew he would love her forever, no matter if she loved his brother or not. The cruel irony stung.

He held her away from him. "You better get cleaned up and go see your dad. I'll see you later."

She reached up and kissed his cheek. "Thank you, Quincy." She walked away, her wet sneakers squeaking on the shiny hospital floor.

It was after eight o'clock when he climbed

back into the truck. He found his phone in the backseat and he supposed his jacket and slicker were in the ER. It didn't matter. He had others.

Checking his phone, he saw he had seven messages: two from his mother, two from Elias and three from Grandpa. Evidently, he'd been missed. First, he called his mother to let her know what had happened, then he called Elias because his grandpa would never get off the phone. Elias told him he'd already picked up the soup so Quincy headed home.

Grandpa met him at the door loaded with a ton of Rebel drama. "Where have you been? I've been worried sick."

Quincy was soaked and cold and he was not in a mood to listen to Grandpa running on. "I told Elias what happened." He walked into the house.

"You couldn't call?"

He turned to face his grandpa. "Clyde was lying out there on the cold, hard ground, barely alive. No, I didn't have time to pick up the phone and call my grandfather. I was worried the man wouldn't make it."

Grandpa sagged and all of his seventy-six years showed in the wrinkles on his face. "I thought something had happened to you. I can't lose a grandson, especially you."

He threw an arm around his grandpa's shoulders. "I'm fine. I'm a little wet and tired, but fine."

"Don't scare me like that again."

"I'll try not to. Now I need a shower and some dry clothes." He made his way down the hall to his room. As he was pulling on some jeans, Elias came into the room.

"Grandpa was really shook up when we couldn't find you. He made me go three times to your barn to check on you. The fourth time he went with me and we opened up the barn and looked around to satisfy him. Your truck was there, but you weren't. He was afraid something had happened to you."

Quincy slipped on a fresh T-shirt. "I know. I called as soon as I could."

"Don't do that to us again. I'm not equipped for this."

Quincy slapped his brother on the back. "You did great. Is any of that soup left?"

"Grandpa wouldn't let me eat all of it. He saved you a big bowl and some bread pudding," Elias said on their way to the kitchen.

Quincy put the bowl in the microwave to warm up the soup. "I'm going back to the hospital in a little while. Do you think you can handle Grandpa?"

"Quincy." Elias sighed deeply.

"I don't want Jenny to be alone."

Elias lifted an eyebrow. "Ah, Jenny. Sweet Jenny."

"Will you stop trying to read my mind and stop goading me?"

"I don't read at all, big brother. I just go by the signs. Anyway, isn't Lindsay there?"

Quincy took the bowl out of the microwave and sat at the table. "Yeah, but they're both upset and worried and Lindsay has a tendency to pounce."

Elias straddled a chair. "Now, there's a woman who's wound too tight. I bet she doesn't even have to curl her hair."

"Do you know everything about every woman in this town?"

"Just about. That's why they call me The Stud."

Quincy spit soup all over the table.

"Hey, I'm serious."

"Since when?" Quincy took his bowl to the sink. Everyone should be as free and uninhibited as Elias. There would be a lot less heartache.

Elias pointed a finger at him. "You tell Grandpa where you're going."

"Tell Grandpa what?" Grandpa shouted from the living room.

Quincy frowned at Elias and then made his way there. "I'm going back to the hospital to check on Clyde."

"Now? In this weather? You just got home." Mutt was comfy in his bed by Grandpa's chair. Evidently, the dog had opted for the warm house instead of the freezing weather.

"Clyde's in bad shape and I'm worried about Jenny."

Grandpa shook his head. "Boy, that's just asking for trouble."

"It's my life."

Elias plopped down on the couch. "When did you realize that?"

"About two hours ago." The moment Jenny had rested her head on his chest, he'd known there was no turning back for him. Like a poker game, he was going all in, heartache and all.

Quincy finished dressing and found another

coat. In the living room, he spoke to his grand-father. "I'll call a little later. Elias will be here and he'll fix your breakfast."

"We're having cereal, Grandpa," Elias said.

Grandpa thumbed toward Elias. "He's lazy."

"You better not complain. I'm all you got right now."

"Humph" was Grandpa's response to that. "What was Clyde doing out in this weather?"

"He has the same disease you have. It's called Stubborn Pigheadedness."

He pointed at Quincy. "Watch how you talk to your grandpa."

Quincy squeezed his grandpa's shoulder. "I always do."

"Tell Jenny and her sister I'm praying for their dad."

"I will."

Quincy opened the door and a gust of cold air hit him right in the face. It might be presumptuous of him to go back to the hospital, but he knew he wouldn't sleep worrying that something could happen to Clyde. Jenny might need him.

Like Elias had told him, which he found strange since he never listened to his brother: he was going after what he wanted.

Chapter Twelve

Jenny was restless and couldn't sit. She paced in the waiting room while Lindsay talked to the nurses. They were waiting for the doctor to come out and tell them what was wrong with their dad.

So many emotions churned inside her, and through all of them she was cursing herself for not being more assertive and not letting her dad leave the house in bad weather. Lindsay would have put up a fuss and her dad would have stomped off to the living room as he usually did when Lindsay confronted him. But Jenny couldn't talk to her father like that.

She was filled with guilt. It was her fault her dad was injured. How was she going to live with that? She paced some more, wearing out the sneakers Nurse Denise had graciously loaned her. How she wished Quincy was here.

She stopped in her path as a stubborn-ass truth hit her. For years she'd been avoiding her feelings for Quincy. Even a child could probably have seen how she felt about him. She went to Rebel Ranch because of Quincy, not to visit the horses, and certainly not to see Paxton.

She ran her fingers through the tangled wet rattails of her hair. *Don't do this. Don't do this*, she repeated to herself. Not now when she was worried and upset. But she knew how she felt. Her future was with Quincy. How did she convince him of that?

Lindsay was coming down the hallway and Jenny ran to meet her.

"What did the doctor say?"

"From the cardiac test and blood work, they've

officially ruled out stroke and a heart attack. And the tests reveal no bleeding or swelling of the brain. They've concluded, as we thought, that from the bruise on his head he must've fallen. They're waiting for him to wake up before doing more tests."

"What about his hip?"

"The X-rays show no fractures or broken bones."

"Thank God. When can we see him?"

"The doctor will be out in a minute." Lindsay sat in one of the chairs and buried her face in her hands. That shook Jenny. Lindsay was very good at controlling her feelings.

She sat by her sister. "What are you not telling me?"

Lindsay raised her head. "I'm just upset that we're not taking better care of our father."

Jenny drew back. "You mean you're upset with me."

"I didn't say that."

"You didn't have to." Jenny got to her feet. "I'm not treating him like a kid, Lindsay. He's a grown man and I'm not going to make him feel helpless and worthless. Yes, I regret that I didn't go with him and I'll probably regret that to the day I die. I'm well aware this is my fault."

"Jenny…"

The doctor came out and Lindsay was immediately on her feet.

"Your father is awake and asking for you. He's got a few things mixed up in his head and he just wants to make sure his daughter is okay. Please only stay a few minutes. He really needs to get his rest."

Jenny hurried into the unit and to her father's bed. She paused when she saw his face. Near his right temple was a big bruise and it was black-and-blue all the way to his eye. His skin was as white as his hair, and Jenny swallowed a sob that threatened to bring her to her knees.

With strength she didn't know she had she

walked closer to the bed. "Daddy," she whispered and leaned down to kiss his cheek.

He opened his eyes and she was never so happy to see his beautiful blues. "There's my girl," he murmured.

"How are you?"

"I'm all right. I feel a little foolish, but that's what happens when you have a hard head."

"Oh, Daddy." She gently hugged him.

"I saw your mother."

"What?" She wasn't sure she'd heard him correctly.

"I could see that mother cow by the woods, and if I drove my truck any closer she'd take off, so I got out slowly and made my way to her. I could see she'd had the baby in the bushes. The calf was okay so I started back to my truck and realized the sky was dark and it was fixing to rain. I guess I got in too big of a hurry. I tripped on a tree root and fell. That's the last thing I remember until I woke up and I was shivering from the cold. I kept trying to get up, but I couldn't, and I thought I would die out there. I guess I was fading in and out of consciousness. Then suddenly your mother was there. I could see her so clearly and she said, 'Not now, Clyde. It's not your time.'"

Tears filled Jenny's eyes and she tried her best not to cry, but she was losing the battle. Lindsay stood on the other side of the bed with a stone-like expression Jenny didn't understand.

"I wanted to go with her and she said no again and that Jenny was coming, and she told me to hold on. It was so cold, but I could feel her presence right there with me. Then I remember you pulling on me and the rain and I tried to wake up to help you, but couldn't. Then your mother's voice said, 'Don't worry. Quincy's coming.'" He looked at Jenny. "Did Quincy come?"

"Y-yes, Quincy put you in the truck."

Lindsay motioned to a nurse and walked over and spoke to her. The nurse nodded and came back with a syringe. She injected the medication into the IV in her father's arm and soon he was out again. Jenny followed Lindsay into the waiting area, fuming.

"Why did you do that? He was talking and he didn't say he was in pain."

"He was talking crazy. Seeing Mama? He was just dreaming and when he wakes up he probably won't mention it again. Rest is what he needs now."

"He needs you to stop being such a hard-ass."

Lindsay's eyes narrowed. "Don't start with me, Jenny."

Jenny went over to a love seat and sat down. She was exhausted beyond anything she'd ever felt, and arguing with Lindsay wasn't going to make things better.

"I'm going to my office to get some rest," Lindsay said. "This would be a good time for you to go home and do the same thing."

"I'm not leaving Daddy."

"Suit yourself."

It was dark outside and Jenny had no idea what time it was. Then she saw the clock on the wall. Almost midnight. What a long night it had been. She curled up on the love seat, just needing a break to regroup. Heather, one of the nurses, brought her a pillow and a blanket.

"Thanks," Jenny said. "When my dad wakes up again, would you please call me?"

"Will do."

Jenny stared into space, unable to sleep. A nurse from the ER came into the room with Quincy's slicker and coat. "Jenny, I don't mean to disturb you, but what would you like me to do with these things?"

Jenny sat up. "I'll take them."

"How's your dad?"

"He woke up, but he's sleeping again. He's going to be okay."

"That's great. Try to get some rest."

Jenny laid Quincy's slicker across the love

seat and curled up holding his coat. It had a musky, male scent that reminded her of him, his warmth, his gentle spirit and his strong presence.

She was drifting into sleep and she sensed she wasn't alone. Turning her head, she saw Quincy standing there, as tall and strong as any oak. All of a sudden everything seemed a little brighter. He was here. That was all she needed.

She sat up. "You're back."

He removed his hat, revealing dark hair that tended to curl, especially in damp weather. Sitting beside her he said, "I wanted to see how Clyde was doing."

She held on to his jacket as if it was the one thing in the world that could give her comfort. "It wasn't a stroke or heart attack. He was hurrying to his truck and caught his foot on a tree root and fell. Evidently it knocked him out, but he woke up several times."

The love seat was small and she scooted a

little closer to Quincy, just needing to be near him. "How did you find us?"

"I was closing up for the night and for some reason I looked toward your property and saw the lights."

"What lights?"

"Your truck lights."

An eerie feeling came over Jenny. "I didn't have the truck lights on. I turned them off when I started looking for Dad. I didn't want to run the battery down and it wasn't dark yet and I still could see. I walked and walked until I found him, but there were no lights."

A confused look marred his face. "I saw lights."

"Dad says he saw my mother and she spoke to him saying to hang on, that Jenny was coming. He said he wanted to go with her but she said it wasn't his time. And when I couldn't pull him any farther she told him again to hang on, that Quincy was coming."

"Jenny, that's weird."

"Isn't it? Lindsay says he's talking out of his head because of the hypothermia, but I believe him. I believe my mother was there and…"

"And what?" He gently wiped a tear from her cheek.

"I wanted to see her, too." He gathered her into his arms and she snuggled against him. "I'm a little emotional right now."

"Just go to sleep." He tried to pull the coat from her arms.

"No. I want to keep it."

"Jenny, it's damp."

"I don't care." She rested her face in the warmth of his neck, feeling his strength, and relaxed. So many years she'd tiptoed around her feelings, but tonight there were no restrictions, no boundaries, nothing holding her back. She kissed his neck and whispered, "I love you, Quincy."

He stiffened and then held her a little tighter.

"Please don't say anything. Tomorrow we can discuss it, but for tonight just let me believe that all these feelings I have for you are as real as the sun coming up in the morning and it's always going to be that way."

He kissed the top of her head and she drifted into peaceful sleep. The sound of Lindsay's voice woke her, but she didn't move.

"You're back?" Lindsay said to Quincy.

"Yeah. Have you heard any more about your dad?"

"No. He's heavily sedated and won't be awake until morning. He's talking out of his head and I don't want Jenny listening to that."

"Jenny's not a child."

"You're not going to support her in her belief that Dad saw our mother."

"My relationship with Jenny is based on honesty and the truth."

"The truth is Dad has hypothermia and a concussion and was imagining things because he misses our mother."

"I didn't imagine the lights, Lindsay. That's how I knew someone was out there."

"What are you talking about?"

"Jenny said she turned the truck lights off because she didn't want to run the battery down and she could still see well enough to look for your father. But there were lights."

"She probably just forgot."

"I don't think so. Whatever happened, happened, and I would appreciate it if you'd stop ragging on Jenny. Your dad's going to be okay and that's the main thing."

"Yes. I'll check with the nurses, and it would probably be a good thing if you could get Jenny to go home. Dad is going to sleep through the night."

"Jenny has a mind of her own, and if she wants to stay here that's what she's going to do."

"Whatever."

"My hero," Jenny whispered.

"You're awake."

"Partially. Don't think too badly of Lindsay. She gets that way when she's upset—bossy."

"I was under the impression she was that way all the time."

"Bad boy." She poked him in the ribs and scooted as close as she could get, and it wasn't close enough.

"Go to sleep."

"I will if you will. You once told me you could sleep anywhere."

He pulled the blanket over both of them and settled back into the sofa. "Sweet dreams, Jenny Rose," he whispered.

WHEN JENNY WOKE UP, it was light outside. She stared at the man beside her, his handsome face relaxed in sleep. He had a growth of beard that made him sexier than sexy with his raw-boned features and beautiful eyelashes. They were long and gorgeous. She'd never noticed that before. She wanted to stay wrapped around him forever, but she knew that was ridiculous. Life awaited and she was ready to take her chances on whatever came next because in her heart she knew Quincy would never hurt her. She quickly untangled herself and he immediately stirred.

"I'm going to check on Dad."

In the ICU, her sister was already there talking to the doctor. Her dad was awake and she immediately went to him.

"How are you this morning?"

"Sore and weak."

Jenny stroked his hair. "That will pass. You have two daughters who are nurses and we are at your disposal."

Her dad coughed and Lindsay grabbed a stethoscope and listened to his chest. "I'm fine," her dad grumbled. "Stop fussing over me. I'm ready to go home."

"Not for a few days, Mr. Walker," the doctor

said. "We want to keep a close eye on you to make sure there are no repercussions."

"Ah, okay."

Jenny kissed him and walked back into the waiting room to Quincy. "He's doing much better," she told him. "Do you know where my truck is? I need to go home, take a shower and change clothes."

"I'm driving it. I'm ready when you are."

Her emotions had run the gamut in the past twenty-four hours and she was trying hard to stay ahead of them. But she was positive about one thing. She wasn't ever letting Quincy go. They'd have to talk about the woman in Plano, and she planned to bring up the subject just as soon as they were alone.

SOON THEY WERE on their way back to Horseshoe. Jenny was drained and she knew Quincy was, too. Neither of them had gotten much sleep.

As Quincy turned onto Rebel Road, he asked, "Do you want to just drop me at the ranch?"

"No. I'd rather not be alone right now. Unless you have to go to work or something."

"I spoke to Falcon and told him I wouldn't be in today and the reason for that. He said to tell you he hoped your dad gets better real soon."

"I hope so, too." She turned to face him. "Did Elias tell you we saw each other the other night?"

"Yeah. He said you asked about me."

"Mmm. I was miserable, but I tried to have a good time. Elias asked me to dance and I did because I wanted to hear about you. He said you needed a nurse."

Quincy reached out and touched her arm and she covered his hand with hers. "I do, but not just any nurse—you."

"Aw."

Quincy drove up to the house and she leaned over and kissed his cheek. They got out of the truck and went into the house. A pang of sadness hit Jenny as she walked in. Everything was just as she'd left it. The TV was still on, a roast was on top of the stove waiting to be eaten and the doors were unlocked. She quickly pulled herself together and went to take a shower. She could hear Quincy fumbling around in the kitchen and that warmed her heart. He was here and that was all she needed.

It took a while to scrub all the dirt out of her hair. She wrapped it in a towel because she didn't want to take the time to dry it. She slipped on a big T-shirt and went to join Quincy. Squatted on the floor, he was feeding Daisy.

"Oh, I forgot about poor Daisy."

"She was whining at the back door so I let her in and gave her some of that roast on the stove."

"Thanks."

He stood and eyed her in the T-shirt. "Why don't you get some sleep and I'll check on White Dove and the other horses."

They were talking like polite strangers and Jenny didn't like that. "We need to talk," she said, and walked into the living room and curled up in the corner of the sofa.

He followed and took a seat beside her, looking as nervous as she'd ever seen him. She just wanted to kiss that look away. But first they had to talk.

"Who is this woman in Plano that you see?"

He leaned back on the sofa and relaxed in a way that made her nervous. Placing his hands behind his head, he asked, "Curious, are you?"

"Yes. Why all the secrecy?"

He lifted a dark eyebrow. "There's no secrecy."

"Really? I've never hard anyone in the family talk about her."

His eyes caught hers. "Her name is Wendy."

The name sent a cold chill through her because by the tone of his voice she knew the woman was important to him. She'd never had these feelings about the women in Paxton's life, but now she was feeling green-eyed jealousy because Quincy had known someone else.

"I was in Afghanistan with her son. He was my sergeant and we were close."

All the jealousy dissipated with his words and she waited with bated breath for him to continue.

"He's still in Afghanistan, but he has a small son who has spina bifida and Wendy has a hard time caring for him. The wife left, unable to deal with the boy. Every now and then, I take a weekend off and go and give Wendy a break. She goes out to dinner with friends or to the movies or shopping or whatever she wants to do and I take care of Little Will. He loves horses and I—"

Jenny crawled into his lap, losing the towel around her head in the process, and wrapped her arms around his neck. Knowing Quincy, she should've guessed it was something like that. "You are the most amazing man I've ever known. Your heart knows no bounds."

With one finger she traced the shape of his lips until he caught the end and nibbled on it. She squirmed against him and brought her lips to his. She nibbled and tasted until he captured her lips with an intensity that took her breath away. He pressed his firm lips against hers and her heart jolted in anticipation. At the touch of his tongue, she opened her mouth and kissed him as if she'd never kissed anyone before in her life.

He tasted of sunshine, the outdoors and cowboy, and she floated away on a wave of pure delight as a current of desire ran through her. A current so strong she knew nothing in this world would feel the same again unless she was able to kiss this man just the way she wanted.

She planted kisses on the corner of his mouth, along his jawline and to his ear. "Take me to bed."

"Are you sure about this? Absolutely, positively sure, no doubts, no insecurities, no turning back? This is it." His voice was hoarse and his eyes as dark as she'd ever seen them.

She pulled her T-shirt over her head, exposing her breasts, and smiled. "Cowboy, I've never been more sure of anything in my whole life."

Chapter Thirteen

Quincy cupped her breast, making it difficult for her to think. "First, tell me what you said at the hospital again."

She leaned back in his arms. "What? That Daddy's going to be fine?"

"No, not that."

"That when Lindsay's upset she gets bossy?"

"No, not that, either. Before that."

"Oh." She cradled his loving face in her hands. "I love you. It's taken me a long time to realize that, but…"

His lips captured hers and she melted into everything she ever wanted, not holding back as he deepened the kiss. "I love you with all my heart, Jenny Rose," he whispered against her lips. "I've loved you for so long, but I never could tell you because of Paxton." He stroked her wet hair away from her face. "I don't want this to be out of your need for someone today. I want it to be for real and lasting into eternity."

"Oh, Quincy." She caught his hand and kissed it. "It is. I know you're conflicted about Paxton because he's your brother and you have this honorable streak a mile wide. But I'm not in love with Paxton anymore. You have to trust me on that. He's a friend, that's it. Can you do that?"

"Yes. I decided at the hospital that I was going to fight for you even if I had to use my fists."

She looked into his gorgeous eyes. "You don't have to do that and you don't have to feel guilty, because we're two consenting, single adults." She kissed the tip of his nose. "After my mother died, I was so lonely and sad. I missed her love, and I missed her just being in my life." Her voice cracked and Quincy tightened his arms around her. This was so hard to explain. She didn't want to sound wimpy and needy, but at the moment, that was exactly what she was. She knew Quincy would understand, though. "My dad and Lindsay loved me, but I needed more. I needed to feel loved and I got that from Paxton. It changed over the years, but I kept clinging to that feeling. No matter what Paxton did, I always forgave him because I had this desperate need to be loved. Last night when my dad said he saw my mother, I realized that she really isn't gone. Her presence is always with me and so is her love. I don't need to take crap from someone who always disappoints me. And I won't again. This time, I'm loving for real and all the way into forever with a man I know I can trust. With a man I know will never let me down. With a man I know will love me as much as I love him. Does that make sense?"

He cleared his throat. "Perfectly. I just wanted you to be sure, because once we start this relationship there's no turning back for me. We'll have to tell Paxton. I don't want to have a secret affair. I want everyone to know and I want to be up front about everything."

"Quincy," she murmured and kissed his lips. The moment she did, Quincy relaxed. He loved her, and any guilty feelings he had, he pushed aside for her. He lifted her into his arms and carried her down the hall.

"On the right," she said.

He went through the bedroom door and kicked it shut with his foot. Gently laying her on the bed, he ripped off his chambray shirt. Jenny stood on her knees and ran her hands across his broad shoulders, loving the way his muscles tightened at her touch. She pulled him forward, wanting to savor every morsel of those magnificent muscles. They tumbled onto the bed. After that, it was a frantic effort to get out of unnecessary clothes. Not once did her lips leave his. She couldn't bear to be away from him.

Quincy ran his hands across her body and a warmth charged through her, centering in her lower abdomen with an aching need. His hand massaged her breasts and she thought she would die from the pure pleasure of his touch.

"You're so beautiful," he said in a throaty voice.

She kissed the rippling muscles in his arms. "So are you, cowboy."

Nothing was said for some time as they became acquainted with all those intimate places known only to lovers. His calloused hands were like velvet against her sensitive skin. Nothing had ever felt more erotic.

Her hand found all the hardened planes of his body, and the touch of his roughened skin against hers sent the pleasure meter spiraling out of control. He rained kisses from her breast to her stomach and lower and back to her lips once again. All she could feel was him and all the emotions that he created in her.

When he came to her, she was more than ready. It seemed as if she'd waited all her life for this man to make her his. The coupling was unlike anything she'd ever experienced before. He was gentle yet rough, caring yet thorough and loving with every ounce of strength in his body. Jenny felt it in the spasms that shook her, in the moans that left his throat and the sighs that filled her until there was nothing left but undisguised pleasure.

He rolled away and took her with him. She lay atop him, their sweat-bathed bodies entwined. She'd never felt so relaxed in her whole life, as if her world was complete now. Resting her head beneath his chin, she gave in to the peaceful feeling and went to sleep.

A LONG TIME LATER, Quincy woke up and watched Jenny sleep. Little moans escaped her throat and he found that enchanting. *She* was enchanting. But then he'd been smitten with Jenny Rose for a long time. He'd never thought they would reach this point. But now he wondered why he had waited so long. Paxton had made his choice and Quincy had now made his.

He would tell his brother as soon as he could, because he didn't want him to hear it from anyone else. Paxton was getting married in the spring so it shouldn't be a big deal. But still, Quincy had a hard time with the word *betrayal*.

He reached for the comforter and pulled it over them. Snuggling against him, Jenny sighed and Quincy went back to sleep. The next thing he knew Jenny was shouting at the top of her lungs.

"Quincy! Quincy!" He loved the way she said his name even when she was screaming it.

She ran around the room like a crazed person, pulling out clothes and jumping into them. He rose up on his elbows watching her and he'd never seen a more beautiful sight. Her hair was everywhere; her breasts were round globes of temptation. Her butt was perfectly formed and all he wanted to do was…

"Quincy, get up. It's three o'clock. I have to get to the hospital. We overslept."

He dragged himself out of bed and she threw his shirt and jeans at him. "Oh, this is the way it is, huh? Wham, bam, thank you, sir?"

"Don't tease me." She attempted to pull a brush through her hair, but the tangles were stubborn. "I'm sure Lindsay has called me about fifteen times, but I don't know where my phone is. It has to be out in the pasture somewhere."

Pulling on his jeans, he said, "I'll find your phone and take care of everything around here. Take your truck and go."

"I love you." She ran to him and threw her arms around his neck and he lay back, pulling her on top of him. He held her for a moment just remembering their lovemaking. It had been everything he'd ever wanted, or expected.

"No regrets?"

"No regrets." She kissed him and before he could kiss her back, she jumped up. "If we get started, it'll just make me later. I have to go. Tonight." She winked and disappeared out the door.

"I love you, too," he shouted after her, smiling, and grabbed his shirt from the floor. He stretched his shoulders and smiled. This morning, he'd eased a lot of tension, and he felt more at ease than he had in a long time.

The cold wind nipped at him as he let Jenny's horses out of their stalls and fed them. They were eager to romp in the pasture. He walked to where Clyde's truck was parked near Quincy's barn. It didn't take him long to find Jenny's phone in the mud. It was ruined. He put it in Clyde's truck and drove back to the house.

Then he made his way to his barn to take care of his horses.

Jericho was there, putting sweet feed in a trough. The horses gathered around, stomping in the mud.

"Thanks," Quincy said.

"I finished feeding early and noticed your horses weren't in the pen, so I came over to let them out and feed them."

"I got held up." For the life of him he couldn't stop the silly smile plastered across his face.

"Yeah. I see." Jericho slapped him on the back. "Enjoy it, man."

Quincy walked about six feet off the ground for the rest of the day. He didn't even mind Grandpa calling him three times asking what they were going to have for supper. Elias was right. He'd spoiled his grandfather.

He didn't know how to get in touch with Jenny so he just waited for her to call. The call came about eight that night. She said for him to meet her at the house and he was out the door in a flash.

"Where you going?" Grandpa called.

"I'm going to Jenny's to see if she needs any help."

"What kind of help? It's dark."

Elias laughed and Grandpa turned on him. "What's wrong with you?"

Elias snapped his fingers. "Think, Grandpa."

Quincy wasn't hanging around for this dog and pony show. "I'll see y'all later."

He drove into Jenny's yard as eager as a teenager. It had been a long time since he'd had these feelings. Maybe too long.

Jenny met him at the door in a short bathrobe. She leaped into his arms and her lips caught his in a passionate kiss. The kiss went on and on and Quincy wondered how he ever lived without this.

She wrapped her legs around him and whispered, "Bedroom."

He managed to kick the door shut and they turned and twisted through the living room and down the hall. They knocked something over but they didn't stop to see what it was. They were otherwise engaged.

Quincy had always been a stickler for time, but once again he lost track of it and where he was. They made love. They slept. They took a shower together and time ceased to exist. It was just the two of them and that was enough.

At 5:00 a.m. he woke her up. They dressed in silence, and arm in arm, they made their way to the front door.

"Your phone's in your dad's truck. It's toast," he told her.

"I'll get another one today."

"Call or text me when you do, so I can stay in touch."

She stood on her toes and wrapped her arms around his neck. "I love you." His arms tightened around her and they had a hard time letting go.

"I know you're worried about Paxton…"

"It's almost Thanksgiving, and he and Phoenix are coming home. I'll tell him then. I'd rather not do it on the phone."

"I forgot about Thanksgiving. I'm not sure my dad will be home."

"We'll spend some time together no matter what's going on."

She drew back and smiled. "I knew I loved you for a reason."

He stole another kiss and walked out. He didn't look back because he wasn't strong enough to resist the temptation of going back into her arms.

The next few days were difficult for Jenny. Her father developed pneumonia and she and Lindsay never left the hospital. He looked so pale, and Jenny worried he might not pull through even though the doctors assured her and Lindsay that he was getting better. Her only bright spot was Quincy. He brought her food and he brought her love. The latter was what she needed the most.

On Thanksgiving morning, her father turned a corner. He was awake and talking and Jenny immediately ran to call Quincy, but caught herself in time. She knew he was with the Rebel family because it was a big holiday and she didn't want to interrupt.

Besides, this was the day he was going to talk to Paxton and she worried about that. With Quincy's high moral character, she was nervous about how Quincy would react if Paxton became angry. Sometimes Paxton could be an ass. Well, that wasn't exactly correct. He could be an ass most of the time, but Quincy was a big boy and he could take care of himself.

Lindsay walked into the waiting room. "You look beat."

"Thanks."

"Dad kicked me out of his room. He said for me not to come back for a few hours, so why don't we go home and change and fix something to eat."

"You go ahead. I feel someone still needs to stay here. He's not completely out of the woods yet. When you come back, I'll go." She had a devious plan. The Rebel dinner would be over by then and she might get a chance to be with Quincy.

"I plan to take a long nap."

"Fine."

After Lindsay left, Jenny paced, and she thought this was the most exercise she'd had in a while. Not exactly, she reminded herself, remembering her nights with Quincy. Her long, wonderful nights with a man she loved.

Paxton had called her a prude, but with Quincy she found she wasn't. She was free, uninhibited and brazen and she was going to die if she couldn't see Quincy soon.

She paced. She wanted everything to go smoothly when Quincy talked to Paxton, but she had this eerie feeling she couldn't shake. Quincy was so honorable. Would he go against his brother for their love?

What was going on at Rebel Ranch?

QUINCY'S MOTHER'S KITCHEN smelled of cinnamon, apples and turkey. It reminded him of all the love and happiness they'd shared together as a family. Everyone was there, except Phoenix and Paxton. They were still waiting for them to arrive. Everyone was asking about Jenny's father, but Quincy's attention was on the back door. Where were his brothers?

Everyone took turns holding baby John, even Quincy. John had big dark eyes and he looked around at everybody with a smile. He was a happy baby. But soon Eden took him and handed him off like a football to someone else. There was a lot of laughter and love in the house and Quincy wished Jenny could be there. He missed her.

"Uncle Quincy." Zane approached him. "I'm going to race Bear this afternoon and show Dad how fast he can go. You want to watch me?"

Quincy was hoping to get away and go see Jenny later, but… "Sure, partner. You've been practicing a lot lately."

"I have to. That's how you get better."

"They're coming," Elias shouted. "I see Phoenix's truck."

Grandpa pushed up from the sofa. "About damn time. I'm getting hungry."

"Dinner will be on the table in fifteen minutes, Abe," their mother said. "The girls are setting the table now and the food is ready."

The back door burst open and Phoenix came in. Quincy got to his feet, but Elias was the first to respond.

"Where's Paxton?"

Phoenix plucked a tomato out of the green salad bowl on the bar and popped it into his mouth. "The crazy fool went to California to spend Thanksgiving with Lisa."

This immediately had their mother's attention. "Why didn't he call and inform me of this change?"

Phoenix plucked another tomato and got his hand slapped. "Ouch."

"Why didn't he call?"

Phoenix cocked a hip against the counter. "Well, Mom, you know how he is about phone calls. He knew you'd get mad, and since he's a big chicken, he didn't make the call. He and Lisa are having some issues and he wanted to see her in person."

"What kind of issues?" Quincy asked.

Phoenix shrugged. "Who knows? One minute he's in love and the next minute he's with some buckle bunny."

"He's seeing other women?" Kate asked with her hands on her hips. She wasn't happy. And neither was Quincy. That ingrained habit of making peace reared its ugly head and all the happiness he was feeling took a hit. It didn't diminish anything he felt for Jenny. Nothing would ever change that.

"Ah, Mom, I don't want to answer questions like that."

She stuck a finger in his face. "Tell me what's going on with your brother."

"He's confused and I don't think he knows what he wants. He's calling Jenny again."

The world tilted. For a moment.

Jenny had told him to trust her, and his world righted itself. She and Paxton had a history and they were friends—just friends. Quincy would never interfere with that, so he had to cowboy up. A friendship didn't mean anything else. It was Paxton's charm that gave him pause.

Elias shoved a glass of wine into his hand. "Drink. Don't ask questions. Just drink."

"Why do I need this?"

"You know." Elias gave him a cockamamy grin. "He's baaack."

"That doesn't bother me."

"Oh, yeah." Elias tipped up his wineglass. "And pigs have been known to fly. Don't fool yourself, big brother. A showdown is coming and you better be packing every weapon in your arsenal because it's not going to be pretty."

"Love is about trust."

Elias laughed hard, slapping his leg and almost spilling his wine. Their mother gave him a sharp glance and Elias sobered immediately. "Love, huh? You're finally admitting you love her? But love's about trust? That's pure Quincy and pure bull you-know-what."

"Shut up." Quincy thought it funny that tough Elias never cursed in front of his mother.

"Now, listen up. This is truth and fact. I know

Paxton. You know Paxton. If he's breaking up with Lisa, you can bet every dollar in your pocket he's coming back for Jenny. It's a tradition with him."

"Are you drunk?"

"Not yet, but I plan to be by the time the sun sets tonight. All this family togetherness is a load of you-know-what. I'd rather be drinking down at Rowdy's with women who appreciate me."

"Why don't you go tell Mom that."

"I don't have a death wish."

Elias was one of the hardest-working men Quincy had ever known, but his views on life were attached to a beer bottle and easy women. Elias had to find his own way, just as all the brothers had. Sometimes it wasn't easy for any of them.

"Just remember what I told you." Elias said as he walked off to get another glass of wine.

Dinner was a fun affair with lots of talk about

the holidays. Of course, baby John was the center of attention, sitting in a high chair between his parents. Elias and Phoenix got into an argument over the last piece of pumpkin pie. While they argued, Grandpa ate it. Their mother saved the day by bringing out another pie. Everyone was happy.

Later that afternoon, Quincy walked with Jude and Zane to the barn. Zane was as excited as Quincy had ever seen him. He saddled Bear, talking nonstop. They all left the barn to prepare for the race.

Jude had a stopwatch. "Okay, son, when I say 'three,' go. One, two, three."

On the count of three, Zane dug in his heels and Bear responded and off they flew toward the cattle guard.

"I wouldn't read too much into what Phoenix said." Jude had picked up on his mood.

"I'm not."

"You are," Jude contradicted him. "You were

all happy and now you look as if somebody let the air out of your tires."

Quincy was dealing with a lot of conflicting thoughts and he didn't want to share or talk, but he found himself saying, "I trust Jenny."

"Good for you. They have a history and it's hard to wipe that away. Doesn't mean she still cares for him or loves him. It just means they're talking."

"I know that."

"If you're feeling any doubts, talk to Jenny. Take it from someone who didn't talk when he should have." His brother was talking about his affair with Zane's mother. "I should've told Paige I didn't want to give the baby up. I should have voiced my opinion. Now she doesn't know our son is with me and I don't know how I'll be able to tell her if she comes back to Horseshoe."

"That's probably not going to happen."

"Yeah. She left us behind a long time ago and my wish is that she stays wherever she is."

Zane zoomed past them, Bear's hooves barely touching the ground. Zane trotted the horse to them. "Did you see?"

Quincy watched his nephew's excitement and he was happy for him. Inwardly the doubts were about to kill him. He'd told Elias that he trusted Jenny. Now his faith would be challenged. But he couldn't get the thought out of his head: If Paxton wanted Jenny back, what would she do?

Chapter Fourteen

Jenny checked her phone to make sure she had it on. The hospital frowned on cell phones, but this one time she ignored the rules. Quincy should've called by now. It was late afternoon and the Rebel dinner was over, so why hadn't he called?

A bad feeling settled in her stomach. What if he and Paxton had gotten into a fight? That wasn't Quincy, though. The Rebel brothers were known for fighting, but Quincy was the peacemaker and he rarely resorted to violence. So why hadn't he called?

To ease her distress, she went to check her

dad. He was sleeping peacefully and his vitals were fine. Even his color had improved. Soon they would be able to take him home. She went back to the waiting room to stare at her phone. When it rang, she almost jumped off the sofa.

Glancing at the caller ID, she frowned. *Paxton. Ignore it.* It kept buzzing. What if it was about Quincy? She clicked on.

"Paxton, why are you calling me again?"

"I need someone to talk to."

Jenny sat back on the sofa. "Don't you have a fiancée?"

"That's the problem."

Jenny didn't want to hear this and she didn't know why she didn't just click off. She wanted to hear how it had gone with Quincy, though.

"You need to talk to Lisa, not me."

"That's what I'm trying to do. I came out to California to talk to her and she's with some casting director and I'm sitting in her apartment waiting."

Jenny leaned forward. "You didn't come home for Thanksgiving?"

"No."

"Did you call your mother?"

"No."

"Paxton, you know how she is about the holidays. She's going to be so upset you didn't call."

"I know. I'll call her in a few minutes."

Paxton was selfish and uncaring and she saw that now more than ever. He only thought about himself and his needs.

"Did Phoenix come home?"

"Yes, and he's mad at me, too. We're going to Vegas in a few days and my riding is off because I can't stop thinking about Lisa."

"I can't help you with that nor do I have the inclination to try."

"She wants me to stop riding the circuit and get a job. You know, Jen, the rodeo is my life. I'd be miserable in a job."

She could almost feel Paxton's pain. He loved rodeoing.

"I'm sure you can work something out. If you love each other, there's always a way." She couldn't believe the words coming out of her mouth. But they'd been friends for a long time. She knew what true love was now and she felt bad his life was falling apart.

"I hate it out here. There're no horses or wide-open spaces unless you travel for miles."

"Just talk to Lisa. I really have to go."

"If she was here, I would. Who gets a casting call on Thanksgiving?"

"Did you call her?"

"Yes, and she said she'd be home shortly."

"There's your answer. You just have to wait. Goodbye, Paxton. Call your mother. You really need to think about others every now and then."

"Don't preach to me."

"Fine." She ended the call. She didn't want to listen to Paxton's problems. Cradling her phone, she murmured, "Quincy, why aren't you calling?"

AFTER JUDE AND Zane went back to the house, Quincy saddled up Red Hawk. The horse needed exercising and Quincy needed to get away with his thoughts.

He'd call Jenny when he got back. Right now he just needed some time alone to deal with the turmoil in his head. Before he could swing into the saddle, Grandpa walked into the barn and eased onto a bale of hay, chewing on a toothpick. "Wondered where you went. Jude said you were out here and I thought I'd come and see what we're gonna do for supper, eat at home or over at your mom's?"

Yep, he'd created a monster. But it wasn't so much that as it was his grandfather needed someone and Quincy was that someone. Everyone needed somebody.

"Mom has all that leftover food and it would be silly of us to cook more. Besides, I'm not all that hungry."

Grandpa shook his head. "Boy…" He had a look on his face as if he wanted to hug Quincy.

He put his boot in the stirrup and swung into the saddle. "I'm fine." Red Hawk pranced around, wanting to run. "I'll catch you later."

"Quincy…"

He pretended not to hear and shot out of the barn. He gave Hawk his lead and the cool November air embraced them as they flew over winter coastal fields and wide-open spaces. It was invigorating and freeing, and it was what he needed to think clearly.

Sometime later, he rode back into the barn, unsaddled Hawk and rubbed him down. As he led the horse to his stall, Jenny walked in. Quincy's heart lifted at the sight of her. He hated he had doubts. He loved her, and that was all that was important.

"How's your dad?" he asked, as she went into his arms.

"Much better. We're taking turns sitting with

him. Lindsay's with him now and I have the whole night free. I've been calling and calling to tell you that, but you haven't answered."

"I was giving Hawk a workout."

She moved away, eyeing him. "Something's wrong. You're tense. Why?"

He sat on a bale of hay and she took a seat beside him. No touching. No smiling. The temperature in the barn dropped a few degrees. "Paxton didn't come home for Thanksgiving." He glanced at her then and saw the flash of guilt on her cheeks. "But you know that already, don't you?"

"Yes." She clasped her hands in her lap. "He called me. He and Lisa are having some problems and he's under the impression that I could help him."

"Phoenix mentioned he's been calling you."

"I wasn't trying to hide it. Does that bother you?"

"I thought it wouldn't and it has surprised me

that it does. I'm not proud of that and I'm struggling to handle it."

"Why? I told you I don't love Paxton anymore. Why don't you trust me?"

"I'm trying to figure that out myself. I think it has to do with the fact that you and Paxton have a history of getting back together. Somehow I just can't ignore that."

"Quincy…"

"Paxton's a charmer. He's charmed you many times. If he breaks up with Lisa and then says he still loves you and wants you back, can you honestly say you know your answer?"

She tossed back her hair. "You're not going to believe anything I say. You said you trusted me, but you don't. You have doubts and that's not love, Quincy." She got to her feet, her dark eyes glittering like bits of hot charcoal.

He stood, too, feeling a load of guilt pressing on his chest. "Be honest, Jenny. You have to see Paxton face-to-face to know what you're really feeling. You say you're friends, but it might be different when you see him. I love you and I'm trying to—"

"You said you would fight for our love, but this isn't fighting. This is giving up." She ran out of the barn, her dark hair flying behind her.

Quincy sank onto the bale of hay and buried his face in his hands. His insides caved in and he fought to draw a breath. What had he done? He'd just lost the most important person in his life.

JENNY RAN INTO the kitchen, tears streaming down her face, and stared at the wine, chocolates and pizza she'd brought for their special Thanksgiving. It was over. How could he do this? She loved him. Why couldn't he believe that?

Wiping away tears with the back of her hand, she tried to understand, but all she felt was the pain in her heart. Paxton's calls meant nothing to her. To Quincy they did. Why did he have to be so damn honorable?

She'd known from the start that Quincy would choose his family over her, but she loved him and she never realized how much until she spent those nights in his arms. Now there was no going back.

Daisy whined at the back door and Jenny let her in. She opened the bottle of wine. "I'm going to have a party all by myself. Do you want to join me?"

Daisy barked.

"It's a poor, poor, pitiful me party. Bring all your heartaches, bring all your tears, because I'm going to drown them tonight in this good vino and tomorrow I won't remember who Quincy Rebel is. I won't care, either." She tipped up the bottle for a swallow. "If you believe that, well, I'll sell you a pocketful of dreams worth…" She choked back sobs and ran to her bedroom.

Daisy followed and barked.

Jenny patted the bed and the dog jumped up. Jenny wrapped her arms around Daisy and held on as if her very life depended on it. A long time later, after she'd soaked Daisy's coat with her tears, she sat up and vowed off Rebel men for the rest of her life.

It was just too hard.

QUINCY CURSED HIMSELF and snapped at anyone who spoke to him. He'd ruined the one good thing in his life. Maybe because of his insecurity about Jenny's love or maybe because of Paxton. It was a devil of a situation and the devil certainly had hold of him.

He worked from sunup to sundown, taking on most of the feeding because he needed hard labor to block Jenny from his mind. Not that he wanted to block her, but he had to find peace of mind some way. He soon found there was no peace. If he wanted Jenny, he had to trust in their relationship, no matter what. That was the cold, hard truth. Even if she talked to Paxton. Even if she said she still had feelings for him. Even if she said there wasn't a chance for them, he still had to hang in there because his heart was on the line and he had to fight for that. Fight for them. Family loyalty and his love for Jenny battled for dominance in his mind. He knew there wasn't much of a choice. He loved Jenny and he had to step up and trust her.

As he drove into town with Elias and Jericho to pick up mineral and salt blocks from the feed store, he realized it wasn't about the phone calls. It wasn't about trust, either. It was about if Jenny really loved him. There it was. They'd jumped into their relationship so quickly and then Clyde had been hurt and they'd been thrown together. Jenny had needed someone and he was there. If he hadn't been there, he wondered if Jenny would have ever said she loved him. Even if she would have recognized it. That was the crux of his problem.

He backed up the truck and trailer to the loading dock at the feed store. Jericho and Elias helped the store employees stack the blocks into the bed of the truck and onto the flatbed trailer. Quincy jumped off the trailer and noticed Jenny standing at the other end of the feed store talking to Axel McCray. What was she doing talking to him? She didn't even like the McCrays.

As he watched, she placed her hand on Axel's arm. A light went off in his head, similar to a lightning bolt, jarring him. Jenny was a nurturing, loving person and everyone in Horseshoe knew that. If someone from the town had surgery in her hospital, she always checked on them to make sure they were okay. So something must be wrong with Axel or someone in his family for Jenny to be so comforting to him. It didn't matter who the person was, Jenny was always there for anyone in need or anyone who had health problems. Or just any problems. Like Paxton.

There are none so blind as those who will not see. An old saying hit him right between the eyes. The green-eyed monster had a strong hold on him. He wanted all of Jenny, not just a part of her. Standing there in the cold winter's day, he realized Jenny belonged to a lot of people. But he had her heart. He was positive of that now. She didn't have to tell him. He knew it.

They climbed back into the truck and headed for the ranch. "Did you see Jenny?" Elias asked.

Quincy pulled onto the highway. "Yes. I saw her."

"Why didn't you go over there?"

"She was talking to Axel, and I'm not all that fond of talking to a McCray."

"Nah. It's something else. What's going on with you?"

"Nothing." He wasn't talking to Elias about

the mess he'd made with Jenny by not trusting her. Or not believing that she really loved him. The only person he was talking to was Jenny.

"Axel's baby is real sick and he's probably talking to Jenny about it."

"How do you know that?" Quincy had known it had to be something like that.

"I get all my information at Rowdy's and it's accurate."

"Yeah, right."

"Stop at Rowdy's. I want a beer."

"We have beer at home."

"I like the atmosphere at Rowdy's."

"I'm not stopping. We have a lot of work ahead of us at the ranch."

"Tell you what." Elias was in his bargaining mood. "If you stop, I'll stay in with Grandpa tonight and you can go see Jenny."

That was the smartest thing Elias had said all day. Probably his whole life. Quincy had to see Jenny and he had to do it as soon as possible.

"Deal." He pulled into the parking lot of the beer joint and they got out and went inside. They ordered and sat at a table near the bar. The place was almost empty that time of day. The old hardwood floors and wooden tables and chairs had seen better days. Neon beer signs decorated the back of the bar and posters signed by country music singers hung around the walls. The ancient jukebox in the corner still spat out songs from as far back as the '60s. The place had an ambience of bygone days.

A couple Quincy didn't recognize was cuddled up in a corner of a booth, and Axel McCray sat at the bar nursing a beer. How had he gotten here so quick? Since a waitress wasn't on duty, Quincy got up to get the cold drafts that Bob had poured.

Axel didn't even make a comment as Quincy stood there waiting for Bob. He seemed to be in another world. Quincy sensed the man was hurting. It was none of his business and he should just walk away. Another encounter with a McCray was not on his to-do list.

But something stronger than his common sense made him say, "You look as if you have the weight of the world on your shoulders."

Bob, a former marine and built like a Sherman tank, tensed, pulled out his cell phone and laid it on the bar. It was a warning: no fighting or else. He probably had the sheriff on speed dial.

"Get away from me, Rebel. You don't know nothing."

"I know a man when he's hurting."

"What's it to you?" Axel kept rubbing the frost off the can with his thumb, not looking at Quincy.

"Nothing." For some reason Quincy still didn't walk away. He reached for the beers and stood there for a moment.

"My baby may not make it through the night. She has a fever of a hundred and six, but Jenny said the medication is working and she'll get better. Jenny knows that kind of stuff."

"Yeah, she does. I hope your baby gets better." Quincy had a surreal moment standing there talking to a McCray and feeling his pain. It was like an outer space–type thing. Unreal. It humanized the enemy, as he had always thought of the McCrays.

Axel didn't respond. He just kept staring at his beer and Quincy wondered what he was doing in a beer joint instead of at the hospital with his child.

Quincy went back to Elias and Jericho with the beers. "What were you saying to Axel?" Elias asked.

"Just getting a glimpse into the lives of the McCrays."

"Is that a 3-D movie?" Elias asked, and then drank his beer. Gunnar came through the door and glanced at them briefly and then went to his brother.

"What are you doing? Your wife has been looking for you. The baby's temperature is dropping. She's going to be okay. Let's go."

Axel stumbled off the stool with tears in his eyes. Quincy sympathized with the man. It had to be rough facing the loss of a child. He didn't wish that on anyone, not even a McCray.

Quincy got to his feet. "Let's go. We have work to do."

"I'm not ready," Elias said.

Jericho grabbed Elias by the back of his collar and lifted him to his feet. "You're ready."

"Damn, Jericho, you don't have to get rough."

As they walked to the door, Bob said, "I guess there's a first time for everything. The Rebels and McCrays in here at the same time and not even a bad word spoken. There's hope for the future."

Quincy nodded as they went out the door and once again they headed for home. On the way Quincy kept thinking about Jenny. Even a

McCray knew to believe her because Jenny was that kind of person. She didn't lie. She didn't exaggerate. She told the truth.

And he had to be the biggest fool who'd ever lived.

Chapter Fifteen

Jenny was having a bad day. The McCray baby was critical and she felt for the family. A bacterial infection for a six-month-old was rough. She wasn't a fan of the McCrays because she'd grown up next door to the Rebels. But she had gone to the feed store to pick up feed and Axel had asked to talk to her. She didn't hesitate because she knew his baby was sick. To ease his mind she'd called the hospital and talked to the nurses caring for the McCray baby. The nurse assured her the baby was getting better but the McCrays weren't buying that. So Jenny had tried to console Axel and reassure him. She'd just gotten a call from the nurse on duty and the baby's temperature was finally dropping. Good news for the McCray family.

So many things shifted her mind from Quincy. And so many things shifted it back. Good thing she had her dad to care for or she just might break down and cry. She gave all of her attention to her dad and his recovery. She wasn't giving up on Quincy, but she recognized that they both needed time. They'd rushed into the relationship and now it would be tested. If it was real like she believed deep in her heart, it would survive.

The National Finals Rodeo in Las Vegas was getting underway the first week in December and Paxton called again. She didn't think twice about answering. Paxton would find a way to talk to her. If she kept pounding it into his head that he didn't matter to her anymore, he would get the message.

"Are you going to watch?"

"Probably not. I spend all my time at the hospital and when I'm not there, I'm sleeping."

"Why are you working so much?"

Paxton didn't know about her father. Paxton's life revolved around him. She told him what had happened in hopes that he would stop calling her.

"Ah, babe, you should have called me."

"Why would I do that? You seem to be under the impression that we're still together. We're not."

There was silence on the other end for a moment. "I know. It's my fault."

"Yes. It's your fault, but it was time for us to go our different ways. Way past time."

"Lisa and I are trying to work things out."

"I hope you do. And please stop calling me."

"Are you going to watch the finals?"

"I don't really have time."

AFTER SUPPER, QUINCY went to the hospital to see Clyde in hopes that Jenny would be there and she would listen to what he had to say. He knew the ICU visiting hours and he was there right on time, but Lindsay was there instead of Jenny.

"You just missed Jenny," Lindsay said. "She's gone up to the pediatric ward to visit with the McCray family and to check on the baby."

"Do you mind if I see your father?"

"No. Actually, he's asked about you a couple of times." Lindsay was being civil, and that meant Jenny hadn't told her about what had happened. He wanted to see Jenny so bad he actually ached from the thought. If he hung out there long enough, he'd get the chance.

Clyde lay in bed, very pale with tubes in his arms and on his chest. When he saw Quincy, he smiled and Quincy knew the man was going to be okay.

"Quincy, it's good to see you."

Quincy shook the man's trembling hand. "Just wanted to see how you were doing."

"Better, but I feel like an old fool."

"It happens to the best of us." Quincy knew that better than anyone. "You don't have to worry about your cows or feeding. I'll take care of it."

"I appreciate that, but you know I have two bossy, determined daughters. Don't know how that happened. Their mother wasn't bossy."

Quincy would have to agree about Lindsay. "I think Jenny is more caring than bossy."

"Yeah, she's my sweetheart. She tries to help everybody. She's worried about the McCray baby, and that's where she is now if you're looking for her."

"I'll catch her later."

"As I was saying, my daughters have the feeding under control, but I appreciate the offer. And thank you for being there when we needed someone."

"You're welcome."

Quincy hung out in the waiting area hoping Jenny would come back, but at eleven o'clock he had to admit she wasn't. And it was too late to stop at the house, so seeing Jenny was put off to another day.

THE NATIONAL FINALS RODEO had started and Quincy, Elias and Grandpa watched every night. Phoenix was riding well and placing in the money, while Paxton was having a rough time.

"What's wrong with that boy?" Grandpa shouted at the TV. "A two-year-old could ride better than that."

"Ol' Pax has his head in the clouds," Elias answered. "Woman problems is my guess."

By the end of the week Paxton had placed out of the money, but Phoenix won the week and the gold buckle. There was a lot of shouting as the whole family watched the last night. Phoenix made a ride of eighty-nine on a bull named Roller Coaster and won. Everyone celebrated. Phoenix called a few minutes later and they all had the chance to congratulate him. His mother asked about Paxton and found out that indeed Paxton and Lisa were having problems.

Paxton would now come home and Quincy was ready for the fight of his life, because he knew if Lisa was out of the picture, Paxton would go after Jenny big-time.

JENNY FOCUSED ALL her time on her dad. He'd been moved to a private room and a therapist was working with him. Once the pneumonia was under control, he began to improve daily. Jenny was busy, but the heartache inside her seemed to grow, especially with the holidays looming. Her goal now was to get her father home before Christmas.

Paxton called during the finals in Vegas and afterward. Lisa had been supposed to come to Vegas, but at the last minute changed her mind. It had affected Paxton's riding and he was angry at himself and at the world.

He was coming home and wanted to know if they could talk. With everything else on her plate, she didn't want to have a conversation with Paxton. But Quincy was right. To put it all behind her, Jenny had to face Paxton and end whatever they had for good.

A week before Christmas, Jenny and Lindsay brought their father home. He was walking again with his cane and doing well. Daisy was so happy to see him, jumping up and down and barking. He sat in the living room in his recliner, smiling. Now life could get back to normal, or as close as possible.

Jenny managed to get a tree up and did some decorating to get in the mood. As she hung ornaments, she wished Quincy was there, just to share moments like these.

Placing the angel on the top of the tree, she asked, "What do you think, Dad?"

"Beautiful, just like my daughter."

"Ah, you say the nicest things." She climbed

off the ladder and kissed his forehead. "I'm glad we made it home for the holiday."

"Me, too." He turned to look up at her. "Did you know Quincy came to see me?"

"What? When?" Her heart raced.

"A couple of weeks ago, he came to see how I was. I thought you knew. I mean, you two are so close."

She sat on the coffee table and tried to untangle a string of lights, which was like untangling all the doubts in her head. "We hit a bump in the road. Well…that's not exactly true. Paxton started calling me again and Quincy has this notion that I might still be in love with his brother."

"Are you?"

She looked directly at her father. "No. I haven't been for a very long time. I finally let go, but I don't think Quincy is ever going to believe me."

Her father gave her a minute. "You know we

haven't talked about the accident and me seeing your mother. I know Lindsay thinks that's crazy, but I did see her and I needed to see her. All these years, I haven't been able to let go because if I did, that would mean she was really gone. I realized that night as I lay on the cold ground with the rain beating down on me that she's really never gone. She will always be in my heart."

She thought about the light mystery, but decided not to tell him. When he was stronger she would. "Dad, that doesn't have anything to do with Paxton and me."

"What I'm trying to say is that letting go is sometimes hard until we realize it's best for us. You spent a lot of years on Paxton, bad years, years where he hurt you, and years that you cried and cried because he wouldn't call or show up. I don't want to see you go back there. Let him go."

She stopped fooling with the lights and smiled

at her dad. "I have. Trust me, I have." She looped the lights around her neck. "What do you think? Would this work as a necklace?"

"As good as anything I've seen."

The front door opened and Lindsay came in with an armful of groceries. Jenny ran to help her carry them into the kitchen.

"Dad seems happy and the tree looks great, except those lights around your neck need to go on the tree."

Jenny made a face at her sister. "You're in a good mood, and I say that because it's such a rare occasion."

Her sister made a face right back at her. "I was hoping I could talk you into staying in tonight."

"As if I go out so much. Oh." Jenny's eyes opened wide. "You have a date? Is it a full moon or something?"

"Shut up. Dr. Caulfield asked me out to dinner to discuss some nursing issues."

Jenny leaned against the counter. "And you're hoping it's more than nursing issues?"

"I can hope."

Lindsay's career was her life, and she seldom dated because all the interns and doctors were terrified of her.

"Good for you."

"I want to shower and change so I better rush. I brought all kinds of stuff for supper and snacks." She hurried toward the door and then stopped. "How come Quincy hasn't been around lately?"

She hadn't told her sister about Quincy. It was private. Intimate. Only between her and Quincy. But her sister deserved an explanation.

"We had a disagreement."

Lindsay frowned. "About what?"

"He's afraid I might still have feelings for Paxton."

One of Lindsay's eyebrows darted all the way up to her hairline. "And?"

"I'm waiting for him to figure that out on his own."

"Jenny…"

She could almost see all of Lindsay's bossy nature gathering strength like a hurricane. She could never resist putting her two cents in. That was why she was so good at her job. She had opinions and she wasn't afraid to voice them.

Holding up a hand to stop Lindsay's little lecture, she said, "My life. My business. Remember?"

Lindsay shook her head and walked off down the hall. Score one for Jenny. Rarely did Lindsay concede so easily. Dr. Caulfield must be very important to her. *Good luck, sis.*

Jenny was giving Quincy time, but she didn't know if she could get through Christmas without seeing him. Patience was not her strong suit.

ALL QUINCY'S GOOD intentions of seeing Jenny didn't happen. Other things had to happen first, like confronting Paxton. His brother had to know how he felt about Jenny before Quincy could move on.

Things slowed down on the ranch, and mainly they just kept up with the feeding and looking after the herds. Phoenix came home a week after the finals in Vegas, but Paxton still hadn't made it. Instead, he had gone to California again to try to sort out his relationship with Lisa.

Christmas drew near and Quincy went to Plano to see Will, who was finally home. Although he enjoyed visiting with his friend, it was hard because it brought back so many memories of Afghanistan. He took Little Will a gift and told him he couldn't open it until Christmas. By the time Quincy left, the boy had torn off all the paper piece by piece. It did him good to get away, and he was prepared to face Christmas without Jenny.

Zane practiced every chance he got with Bear, and Jude was right there egging him on. Quincy and Jude leaned on the fence and watched as Zane rubbed down Bear for the night.

"He's getting better, isn't he?" Jude asked.

"Yep. He'll be ready for that race and we'll all be rooting for him."

Jude pulled out his phone and looked at the time. "We have to go, Zane. We have to meet Ms. Hurley in thirty minutes."

"You have an awful lot of meetings with the teacher."

"Yeah." Jude grinned and it was a sight Quincy hadn't seen in a very long time.

"You like this teacher?"

"Annabel Hurley. She's blonde, twenty-five and about the prettiest thing I've ever seen. She's taking us out for dinner as a Christmas reward for all Zane's hard work in the tutoring program."

"And you get a reward, too."

"You bet." His brother grinned again and

Quincy slapped him on the back. He couldn't be happier for his brother.

As Jude and Zane left, Phoenix strolled in with a frown on his face. "What's wrong?" Quincy asked, making sure all the horse stalls were closed for the night.

"I need to talk to you."

"Sure." Quincy walked into the barn area. "What's up?"

Phoenix looked down at the tips of his boot. "I did something stupid."

"Really? Isn't that an everyday occurrence?"

"This isn't about my usual goofing off. This is serious."

"Okay." Quincy leaned against a stall. "What is it?"

"I didn't do it on purpose. It just kind of slipped out. Paxton sometimes makes me so mad. He called and was going on and on about Lisa and how it was fine if they broke up because Jenny would be waiting for him. Like she always was. Before I could stop myself, I told him Jenny was seeing you. He's coming home in the morning and I just wanted to warn you. He was fighting mad when I told him. There was no reasoning with him."

As Phoenix talked, Quincy curled his fingers into tight fists. "Don't worry about it. He would have found out one way or another, and it's time it was out in the open. Although Jenny and I are not seeing each other anymore."

"It's not because of Paxton, is it?"

He uncurled his hands and flexed his fingers. "No. It's because of me. I want to be sure she's not still in love with Paxton. So you see, this isn't up to me or Paxton. It's up to Jenny."

"You're just going to let him have her?"

Quincy moved away from the stall and placed an arm across his brother's shoulders. "You think I should fight?"

"Hell, yeah."

Fighting wasn't in Quincy's nature. Even

though he'd been known to break up more fights than he could count. But when it came to Jenny, he wasn't sure what he would do. He just wasn't letting Paxton walk all over her again. That was his bottom line.

At the thought, a revelation warmed his heart. Jenny didn't need him to protect her. She could handle her life on her own. Her strength was one of the things he loved most about her. She could work twelve hours at the hospital, come home and feed cows, cook supper and take care of her dad. That kind of woman wouldn't take any more crap from Paxton.

QUINCY DIDN'T AGONIZE over the problem with Paxton. Whatever happened, happened.

The next morning, they were all in the barn getting ready to start their day. It was a few days before Christmas and it was the only time of year one or two of them took care of the cattle.

"I'm out of here," Egan said. "Rachel's not

feeling well and I'm going home and play nurse."

"She's probably pregnant," Grandpa quipped from his seat on a bale of hay.

"What?" Egan shook his head. "No. She has the flu. It's going around at school."

"Whatever," Grandpa muttered.

"Eden's watching the baby over at Mom's, and Leah and I are going shopping." Falcon glanced around at his brothers. "Who's on duty?"

Elias held up his hand with a smirk on his face. "That would be me, Jericho and Quincy, but I'm not hanging around long. I'm meeting a girl in town early this afternoon and I might not be back for a couple of days."

Grandpa chimed in again, "Phoenix is cutting my toenails, so he'll be busy."

"Grandpa," Phoenix wailed. "My sentence doesn't last forever."

"It ends when I say it ends."

"Yes, sir."

"Zane is out of school and he and Eden are putting up the Christmas tree. I think I'm the referee." Jude made his way to the door.

"Well, Rico—" Quincy nodded at Jericho "—looks as if it's just you and me on work duty."

"Fine with me."

The sound of brake shoes grinding echoed loudly and all the brothers waited as Paxton came charging into the barn. He went directly up to Quincy and his right fist connected with Quincy's jaw. He staggered, but he didn't go down.

Paxton pointed a finger at Quincy, his face red with rage. "You broke the brothers' code. You betrayed me and stabbed me in the back. Jenny is mine and she will always be mine."

Elias started to laugh, big chortles shook his body. "Did you rewrite the code to suit yourself? Last I remember, you embarrassed and humiliated Jenny in our mother's living room."

Quincy rubbed his stinging jaw. "Stay out of this, Elias."

Elias bowed from the waist in a mocking gesture.

Quincy stepped closer to Paxton. "How do you figure Jenny is yours, as if she's some sort of material thing?"

"Jenny loves me and only me, and the sooner you realize that the better off you'll be."

"Let me get this straight. You're marrying someone else and yet you want to keep Jenny on the side. Is that what you think of her? She's some cheap slut you can go to whenever you want?"

"Stay away from Jenny."

"No. I'm not staying away from Jenny just because you've suddenly decided you want her back. A lot has changed since you've been gone."

"Jenny will always love me. When you touch her, she's thinking of me. When you hold her, she's thinking of me. When you make love to her, she's wishing it was me."

That was when Quincy's fist connected with Paxton's jaw. He fell backward into some hay. "Get up," Quincy ordered.

Paxton lay there and he seemed unable to move. His brothers made no move to help. Quincy took a deep breath, surprised by his own actions.

"Dad said…never betray…your brother over a woman. You broke the code, Quincy. I expected that from my other brothers, but not from you."

The fight left Quincy and he stared down at a brother he loved and realized no good could come from any of this. But he wanted to make one thing clear. "I live every day by everything our father taught us. Can you say the same? In the past few years, Jenny has spent more time with me than with you. Where were you on Valentine's Day? Her birthday? How many of them did you forget when you were with other women? And when you did come home, you spent most of your time down at Rowdy's. Jenny is not like an old pair of boots you can claim and come back to when your new ones don't suit you. She's a beautiful, strong woman and she deserves to be treated as such. Until you do, I'm not stepping aside. You got that?"

Paxton staggered to his feet and wiped blood from his lip. "I love Jenny."

That was the first blow to Quincy's chest, but he stood his ground. "Is that why you're marrying someone else?"

Paxton picked his hat up from the ground. "Lisa and I broke up for good, and I'm going over to Jenny's to ask her to marry me. I should've done it years ago, so please, just leave Jenny alone."

The second blow almost brought him to his knees, but he would never show any weakness. He turned toward his horse and swung into the saddle.

"Quincy!" echoed through the morning breeze as his brothers shouted his name.

He urged Aries faster, praying he could out-ride the pain.

Chapter Sixteen

Jenny didn't have to go back to work until after the first of the year. That was one of the perks of having a sister with power. Lindsay didn't give herself the same perks but Jenny understood that meant she would be home to take care of their dad.

Her dad walked into the kitchen, leaning heavily on his cane. His worn jeans and Western shirt hung on his thin body. He'd lost a lot of weight. Jenny was determined to help him gain some of it back.

"I'm gonna sit out on the back porch for a while. If the cows see me, they'll come up to the fence and I can check on them. That black heifer should be springing pretty heavy. We need to watch her."

"I saw her this morning. She's fine."

"Good."

"It's cold out."

"I'll take my jacket."

Jenny didn't want to point out that he'd just gotten over pneumonia, so she followed him to make sure he was wrapped up with his coat, his hat and a scarf around his neck. She didn't want to take away all of his independence. After he was safely in a chair, she went back to fixing lunch.

A knock sounded at the front door and she went to see who it was. People from Horseshoe had been coming by to visit, and she hoped it was someone who would stay and visit with her dad. Miss Kate had come by with a casserole and a pie. Mr. Abe and all the Rebels had stopped in to see how her dad was doing. Everyone, except Quincy. Maybe it was him.

She swung open the door and froze. "Paxton."

"Hey, babe. Can we talk?"

She'd been hoping he'd made up with Lisa and they wouldn't have to have this conversation, but that would be the coward's way out for her. She opened the door wider. "Come in. And don't call me babe."

He sat on the sofa and threw his hat to the other end. Jenny eased into her dad's recliner. There was a bruise on the left side of Paxton's face.

"Did you hurt yourself bull riding?"

"No. Quincy hit me."

"What?" That wasn't like Quincy. "What did you do that would make Quincy hit you?"

Paxton shifted in a nervous gesture. "I said something crude about you. I didn't mean it. I was just upset."

"What did you say?"

"It doesn't matter now. Like I said, I was just angry that he was seeing you behind my back."

"Excuse me? Have you just absolutely lost all your senses?"

"I messed up, Jenny. I screwed up my life and it's all my fault."

She had a lot to say to that, but the ache in his voice stopped her.

Staring at his hands, he added, "I thought I loved Lisa, really loved her, but everything I want is right here in Horseshoe, Texas. Right here in this room."

"Paxton…"

"I know I hurt you, but I love you and I'm sorry for all the bad stuff I've done."

She had no words, so she just let him talk.

"I've worked all these years to become the best bull rider, and I blew it all in Vegas because my mind was on Lisa. The guys are laughing at me and I decided to just come home and put the rodeo behind me." He looked into her eyes. "Let's get married and have that family you've always wanted."

She waited so many years for him to say those words, and now that he had it didn't have the ring of truth that it should.

"Because you have nothing else, so you'll settle for me?"

"It's not that."

She got up and walked over to the sofa and sat beside him. "I think it's exactly that. You want me now because Quincy does. And Lisa's still doing a number on your head. Can't you see that? I'm not the answer to your problems."

"You are." He put an arm around her and pulled her into his side. "I can't go on without you, Jenny."

She rested her head on his shoulder. "You're giving up the rodeo?"

"Yeah."

"To marry and have babies?"

He shifted uncomfortably again. "I'm not too crazy about having kids, but if it makes you happy, that's what I want."

"That's not happiness, Paxton. That's not love." She sat up to look at him. "Your whole world is crashing down around you and you're reaching out to me because that's what you've always done. I've always been there, but now you're going to have to stand on your own two feet. You're gonna have to cowboy up."

"But you're my girl."

She shook her head. "No. I'm your friend. And as your friend, I'm telling you, you need to take some time to get your head straight. Rodeoing is your life, so get back into the game. You had a bad ending to a good season. It happens. Show the world you can be a champion. I have faith that you can do that—without me."

"I don't want to do it without you."

"Paxton…"

He put his arms around her and held her tight. "I need you, Jenny."

Paxton was applying all his charm, just as Quincy had said. Now Jenny knew exactly what he'd meant.

QUINCY RODE UNTIL Aries grew tired. He slipped from the saddle at Yaupon Creek and sat on the cold ground, the north wind tugging at him. The water moved at a steady pace, lapping at the bank. The scent of rain was in the air. He drew up his knees and rested his forearms on them. He'd said he was prepared for whatever happened. He wasn't. He knew Jenny loved him, but when Paxton asked her to marry him, what would she do? He had to trust in their love, which he hadn't done before. He had to keep on trusting until she told him otherwise. But the thought of Paxton and Jenny was cutting into his heart at the moment.

The thud of hooves drew his attention, and he glanced over his shoulder to see Elias ride up. His brother slid down beside him.

"I thought you were meeting a woman?"

"I am. I wanted to talk to you first."

It seemed odd that Elias wanted to comfort

him. Maybe he had a soft side after all. Or it could be Grandpa.

"Did Grandpa send you?"

"Nah. But he's worried."

"I'm fine. I just need some time."

They sat in silence for a moment and then Elias said, "You know, everyone comes to you for advice and you take care of their needs without any thought of your own. It's time to think of yourself."

It wasn't like Elias to be so thoughtful, and Quincy appreciated the gesture, so he chose to be flippant instead of sincere. Sincerity would only make them both uncomfortable. "Have you been nipping at something?"

"Nah. I'm saving that for later." Elias leaned over. "Smell me."

"I'd rather not."

"Come on."

Quincy sniffed and frowned. "Is that vanilla?"

"Yeah. I put it on one time instead of cologne

and believe me, the girls liked it. They were eating it up saying I smelled so good."

"There's no vanilla in our bathroom."

"I keep my cologne in the kitchen so I can grab it as I go out the door because sometimes I forget. One time I was in a hurry and grabbed the vanilla flavoring by mistake."

Quincy laughed. He couldn't help himself. It was what he needed to ease some of the tension inside him.

They both watched the flow of the water, and then Quincy just had to ask because he needed to hear someone else say it. "Do you think she'll take him back?"

"They have a past, and Paxton's going to milk that for all it's worth."

"Yeah." Quincy already knew that.

"But I'm hoping Jenny has learned her lesson."

Quincy did, too. He wanted all of Jenny. All of her heart. Everything. She had to make a clean break with Paxton or there was no future for them.

After Elias left, Quincy went to help Rico with the feeding. In the late afternoon, he drove the tractor into the equipment shed. They'd put out enough round bales to last through Christmas. The weather was taking a turn toward winter, so they'd have to keep a close eye on everything. Rico had checked the fence line on the McCray side and everything was quiet there.

As he walked into the house, Grandpa met him at the door. "Where you been?"

"Working." He headed for the bathroom to wash up.

"I want to talk to you," Grandpa called.

Quincy sighed. The last thing he needed was Grandpa giving him advice, but out of respect he would listen. He washed his hands and his face and went back into the living room.

Grandpa was sitting at the kitchen table.

"Come here." He seemed awfully eager about something.

"I need to give Mutt his pain pill first."

"I already gave it to him."

Quincy pulled out a chair and sat down. Grandpa had a small box in his hand. It looked like a jewelry box. What was that old man up to?

He pushed the box across the table. "I want you to have this."

"What is it?" He made no move to take it and an eerie feeling came over him.

"Your grandma's wedding rings. I wanted to bury them with her, but your dad said I might want to keep them and give them to a grandson one day. That way they would stay in the family. I want you to have them."

"Grandpa, thank you for the gesture, but I'm not getting married."

"You never know."

Quincy didn't want to deal with this. The pain

was enough, and he didn't need his family trying to bolster his courage.

When Quincy made no move to open the box, Grandpa did. There was a platinum antique wedding and engagement ring. Quincy remembered his grandmother wearing them. When she was working, they stayed in a little dish on the kitchen windowsill.

"When we got married, we didn't have much money. We bought cheap gold bands for our wedding. Hers broke one day and she cried like a baby. We had a good calf crop that year so I went out and bought her some nice rings. She cried even more when she opened the box. Jenny's a lot like your grandma. She worked side by side with me for years. I couldn't have made this ranch what it is today without her. She—"

"Stop…" Quincy got to his feet. "Stop this, Grandpa. I'm not marrying Jenny, and right now I'm not sure about anything, but I know I need time alone."

"Okay. Take your time."

Quincy frowned. "Aren't you the one who told me to stay away from Jenny?"

"Ah." Grandpa waved a hand. "Don't be throwing my words back at me. Things have changed and so has my attitude. If you want this girl, you go after her. Paxton will survive."

But Quincy wondered if he would. He went to the refrigerator. "I'll make you a sandwich and then I'm going to the barn."

"Eden brought some pizza over. I'll have that. What are you having?"

"I'm not hungry." Quincy placed the pizza on a paper plate and put it in the microwave. The front door opened and Paxton came in.

Quincy removed the pizza and set it in front of Grandpa, bracing himself for what Paxton had to say.

With his hat in his hand, he said, "I came over to apologize for my behavior today."

"Thank you," Grandpa said instead of Quincy. "I hope you have your head on straight now."

Paxton twisted the hat. "I'm not real sure. All I know is I'm really mixed up." He glanced at Quincy. "Can I talk to you?"

Quincy followed him out to the front porch. Mutt raised his head and then went back to sleep.

"I'm sorry I hit you," Paxton said. "There's a lot going on in my life and none of it is good and I wanted to blame someone." Paxton stared at his hat. "You were right when you told me I should be up front with Lisa. I was so besotted, I couldn't see the real woman behind all that beauty."

Quincy reminded himself to breathe. "Is it over?"

"Yeah. I haven't told anyone this, but she

wanted me to sell my share of the ranch so I could fund her acting career."

"You don't have a share until Mom passes away or she gives it to you before then."

"That's what I told her, and that's when I really saw the true Lisa. It wasn't a pretty sight. I never want to see her again."

"Is that why you want Jenny back?" The words burned Quincy's throat, but he had to ask them.

"Jenny and I had a long talk and we're cool now."

"What do you mean?"

"She forgave me and I needed to hear that." Paxton shoved a hand into a front pocket of his jeans and hunched forward in his heavy winter coat as if the weight of the world was too much for him. Quincy wanted to ease his pain, but for the first time he realized he couldn't do that. Paxton's pain was his own and Quincy had to let him work through it.

"You know Dad always said a Rebel man loves forever and I always thought Jenny was my forever girl, but she's not. She was my first girlfriend, and I'm not sure if I'll ever love deeply like Dad talked about. I don't think I have that capability like Falcon and Egan." He lifted his eyes to Quincy. "And you."

Quincy inhaled a long breath. "Paxton, you messed up in Vegas and the Lisa engagement fell apart. So what? That's life. We all go through struggles. No one gets a free pass from heartache. But you're a Rebel. Pick yourself up and get back to rodeoing. Stop feeling sorry for yourself. You're a damn good bull rider, so go out and prove that to me and to yourself and prove all those naysayers wrong."

Suddenly, Paxton stuck out his hand and Quincy shook it. The wind whipped through the trees with an eerie sound as the brothers made peace. Paxton was the first to speak.

"I didn't mean that about the brothers' code. I was just upset."

"I know."

"Don't worry about feeding or any work on the ranch during the holidays. I got it."

"I'd appreciate that."

Paxton placed his hat on his head. "I'm letting go and moving on. There's a whole world out there and I'm going to find what's right for me. I know now it's not Jenny."

His brother walked off into the darkness, and Quincy stood there for a long time, coming to grips with everything that had just happened. There was no need to ask what had happened between Paxton and Jenny. It was enough to know that he and Jenny had a future, if she could forgive him.

He went back into the house. Grandpa was stuffing pizza into his mouth and drinking beer. He looked up at Quincy.

"Paxton okay?"

"Yeah. I think he is."

"He's a good kid."

The ring box sat on the table and Quincy stared at it for about a minute before he picked it up. Everything he wanted was within his reach. But was it what Jenny wanted?

Chapter Seventeen

Quincy drove over to his barn. As he got out, the cold wind jabbed at him like an ice pick. The temperature was dropping fast. He quickly opened the side door and slipped inside. On the left was his horse stalls and on the right was the barn. He flipped on a small light so as not to disturb the horses. They neighed at his presence.

Sitting on stacked bales of hay, Quincy took the ring box out of his sheepskin-coat pocket. Grandpa's eyes had grown huge when he'd picked up the box on his way out. He hadn't said anything, which was just as well because

Quincy didn't understand why he'd taken it. And here he sat staring at it. It was too soon for any talk of marriage. Feelings had to subside and rational heads had to prevail. Paxton would be okay. He just needed time to figure out the rest of his life.

Jenny needed time, too. He hadn't seen her in so long and he felt as if a part of him was missing. He needed to talk to her and soon. It was Christmas after all.

A sound grabbed his attention. He placed the box on the hay and got to his feet. Was it sleeting? He walked to the back door and slid it open slightly to hear icy rain dancing across the tin roof. Damn! He'd better get back to the house while he could. He turned up his collar, switched off the light and went out the side door to his truck parked at the end of the barn.

As he rounded the truck, a flickering light out in the Walker pasture caught his eye. Was it his imagination? He waited just in case, but everything was dark. Reaching for the door handle, he saw it again, the same as the night Clyde had fallen. But the light was closer to Quincy's barn. Huddled in his coat, with the sleet pelting his hat, he walked toward it. Then it disappeared.

But he could see someone trying to open the double sliding doors. He could tell who it was. *Jenny.* What was she doing out in this weather?

"Jenny."

She swung around. "Oh, Quincy." She sagged against the door. "Quincy." The word came from deep within her. It was almost a cry. "You scared me. I…I…wanted to—" She stood there stammering as if it was a sunny spring day and didn't seem to notice the freezing cold or the sleet peppering them. "Are you ever going to believe I love you and only you?"

The sleet whipped into his face, chilling him to the bone, but it didn't stop the warmth from flooding his heart. "Yes. I'm going to love you no matter what, Jenny Rose." The words came out in a throaty whisper, but she heard them. She ran toward him and he caught her in his arms, holding her tight against him. His lips found hers and they clung together, taking and giving everything they needed at that moment when they both knew their relationship was going to work.

"We have to get out of the weather," he whispered into her neck, and carried her into the barn and deposited her on the hay. He left her long enough to get blankets and a towel out of his office. The smell of horse, hay and dusty blankets surrounded them and Quincy never found it more appealing. "You crazy lovable woman. What were you doing out there?" He gently wiped her hair with a towel.

"I was working with White Dove and I saw your barn light and decided I had to see you. I was almost here when the light went out and then it started to sleet."

"Did you walk here?"

"Yes."

"Jenny." He wrapped a blanket around her and they settled into the loose hay.

"I have to call Lindsay or they're going to be worried about me."

Quincy reached for the phone in his pocket and called the Walker house. Luckily, he still had a signal. He told Lindsay that Jenny was fine and he'd bring her home as soon as the storm stopped.

They sat for a moment in silence. "Warm?" he asked.

"Yes. You're like a heater."

He tucked wet strands of hair behind her ear. "I've missed you, Jenny Rose."

"I've missed you, too." She snuggled closer. "I talked to Paxton. I want to tell you that before anything else is said."

"I did, too."

"He's a mess and doesn't know what he wants."

"He's going through a rough time, but I think he'll be fine."

She snuggled even closer and he could smell the scent he associated with her even though it was dampened by the sleet and rain. "I love you with a deep everlasting love that I've never felt before. Paxton is my friend and he will always be my friend."

He swallowed the lump in his throat. "I wanted every part of you, but I soon realized there are a lot of people who depend on you, even the Mc-Crays. Even Paxton. And you give selflessly of yourself. I know that now. I also know beyond any doubts I have your heart. Completely."

She kissed his neck and opened his shirt, raining kisses along his heated skin. "I love you and you better not ever doubt that again." She nipped his chest with her teeth. "Got it?"

"I love you with every breath I take."

It might have been storming outside, but the sun was shining in his heart, and he gathered her as close as possible. All his dreams had come true, and now all he had to do was love her the way she deserved.

"We're going to do the cha-cha lying down right here in this barn with all the horses watching."

"They can't see us."

"That's a shame." She slipped his shirt and coat from his shoulders. "Because I plan to be loud and noisy and love you like there's no tomorrow."

And she did just that. All Quincy's doubts disappeared and a long time later, he held her beneath the blankets in the hay while the storm ebbed away outside. They even forgot it was freezing. They'd generated enough heat to keep them warm.

"How did you know I was at the door?" she murmured against his skin.

"I saw the flashlight."

She turned to look at him. "I didn't have a flashlight."

"I saw a light."

She rested her head on his chest. "Oh, wow, this is spooky. This is like when my dad fell and you saw the light."

"I thought the same thing."

"I think, and I'll never tell anyone else this, but my mom has been guiding me toward you. She's…"

"Always looking out for you."

"Yeah." She rubbed her face against him. "No one would understand but you."

They lay for a long time amazed and grateful that sometimes life had surreal moments that couldn't be explained.

"What are we going to do about Paxton?" Her hand splayed across his chest, and he caught it so he could focus.

"We had a long talk and I believe he's going to be fine. He's just had a lot of bad stuff happen lately."

"How can we be happy if he's miserable?"

"By being honest and straightforward. He knows how I feel about you. We'll just take things slow." He saw the ring box he'd left on the hay and he stretched out his arm to reach it. "But maybe not too slow."

The moment she saw the box, she squealed, "Quincy!"

"This…"

She took the box and opened it. But it was dark where they were laying and she couldn't see. She jumped to her feet without a stitch of clothing on and ran to where the light was shining.

"Oh, Quincy."

He rose up on his elbows to watch her. Her rounded breasts and curvy body sent his thoughts in another direction. Focus. "Come back here. You didn't let me finish."

She flew back to him and snuggled beneath the blankets. "Oh, heavens, it's cold."

"Because you're naked."

"Are you complaining?"

"No. Never." He removed the box from her clenched hand. "Now. Let's do this the proper way."

She kissed him slowly. "I just want to do it." Then she laughed, and he felt happier than he had in his whole life.

"These rings belonged to my grandmother. They're old and you might want something new and up-to-date. That's what I wanted to talk about."

"Are you kidding me? Those rings are gorgeous, and if you don't ask me in a split second, I'm going to smack you."

He tried hard not to laugh. "I think I'm supposed to be on one knee or something."

"Quincy!"

"Jenny Rose, will you marry me?"

"Yes. Yes. Yes!"

He slipped the engagement ring onto her finger and it fit perfectly. Another surreal moment.

Jenny began to cry, and then she laughed, and then she wrapped her arms around his neck and just held him.

"Tomorrow's Christmas Eve, and we always have a big Christmas party at the ranch. I want you to come as my guest and join the family."

"Are we going to tell everyone we're getting married?" She kissed his neck, his chin and her mouth lingered at the corner of his.

"We'll take it slow, like I said, but I don't see any reason to keep it a secret."

Her tongue stroked his lower lip. "I love you, Quincy Rebel."

"I will always love you," he whispered as he pulled her down into the hay.

Jenny was nervous about Christmas Eve. She wanted everything to be perfect, but in life, hardly anything was, except Quincy. He was beyond perfect and she was floating on a cloud knowing he loved her and she would spend the rest of her life with him.

They had a tradition at their house on Christmas Eve. Lindsay played the piano and Jenny sang Christmas carols. When they were kids, they'd put on skits every year for their parents on Christmas Eve. It sounded idyllic, but Jenny tended to sing like a cat with her tail caught in the screen door. Her parents had loved it, though.

As she sang "Jingle Bells" and acted a little crazy for her dad, she glanced out the window just to say thank-you to whatever phenomena was out there that created the lights for Quincy to see. There was no doubt in her mind it was her mother. A ghost? Something mystical? Whatever, Jenny had her own ideas.

She was late getting to the ranch, but as soon as she rang the bell Quincy opened the door and gathered her into his arms. As his lips found hers, she knew that was where she belonged. In his embrace—forever.

"I like that." She smiled at his Santa Claus hat.

He fitted one onto her head. "It's a tradition around here on Christmas Eve. It started when Eden was small. She insisted, and we would never do anything to disappoint her."

She touched his handsome face, loving his strong features that seemed to have been created with the greatest of care. "It's hard to think of the Rebels as softies."

"We are with the people we love."

"Aw." She leaned against him just to soak up some of his strength. "I guess we better go inside."

"Don't be nervous," he said and took her hand, leading her into the den. A huge tree bedecked in the brightest colors of Christmas stood in the corner. Everyone was milling around with Santa Claus hats on their heads and a drink in their hands. Christmas music blasted from the stereo and Eden, Phoenix and Zane were dancing around and being silly. Everyone welcomed her warmly and she relaxed a little bit.

"Get her some eggnog," Miss Kate told Quincy. He hesitated for a moment and then went toward the big punch bowl on a table.

She was talking to Rachel and Leah when Paxton came over. Baby John was in a baby walker bouncing up and down toward Leah. Falcon was behind him.

"It's like radar," Falcon said. "He can find his mother anywhere."

"Just like his dad." Leah laughed and went to her son. Rachel soon followed and that left her and Paxton alone.

"You look great."

"Thank you."

"And different."

"How so?"

"Mature."

She frowned. "Are you saying I'm old?"

He smiled that smile that used to turn her

stomach upside down. But not anymore. That was the young, naive Jenny. Only one man had the key to her heart now.

All of a sudden the smile faded and he became serious like she rarely saw. "I want to apologize for my behavior, for dumping all my problems on you. I treated you badly over the years, and there's no way to erase that from my mind."

"Paxton…" She placed her hand on his arm. "That's in the past. My wish for you is that you will find someone who will love you the way you deserve."

He gave a mock smile. "I don't deserve too much. I've been a real jackass."

"But there're a lot of people here who love you and support you."

"Yeah." He patted her hand on his arm and too late she realized about the ring. She didn't want him to see it this early.

His eyes opened wide, not in anger, but in joy. "Does this mean…?"

"Yes. Quincy asked me to marry him and I said yes."

He took her in his arms and hugged her. "Quincy will be good to you, because he's the best."

She hugged him back. "Thank you, and I hope we can remain friends."

He drew back. "Always. And I reserve the right to call you every now and then."

"Deal. Just stop calling me babe." She laughed and Paxton joined her. All the tension dissipated from her body. Paxton was okay, and now she could enjoy the man walking toward her with a worried expression on his face.

He handed her a glass of eggnog. "Everything okay?"

"Everything's perfect."

"I want everybody's attention," Egan called from the middle of the room with Rachel by his side. The room suddenly became quiet. "I just wanted to tell everyone that Rachel and I are expecting our first child in August."

"Told you," Grandpa Abe said from the couch as everyone gathered round to hug and congratulate them.

"I already knew," Jericho said proudly, smiling at his friend.

After the excitement died down, Paxton said, "I'd like to apologize to Mom, and the family, especially Quincy and Jenny, for being a jackass the past few months. And I say this with all my heart and deep sincerity, congratulations to Quincy and Jenny."

Phoenix turned off the Christmas music playing in the background and everyone stared at them, waiting for an announcement or something.

Jenny whispered to Quincy, "He saw the ring."

"I wasn't planning to do this tonight." Quincy put his arm around her. "But I asked Jenny to marry me and—"

Everyone began to shout with joy and suddenly they were surrounded by eager bodies waiting to hug and congratulate them.

Finally, Miss Kate gathered everyone around the Christmas tree. "I'm so proud of my boys tonight, especially Paxton. He has proved that he's a true Rebel, his father's son. More babies in the family, and my Quincy has found true happiness. I'm so happy."

As the fire crackled in the fireplace, they sat around, some on the sofas and some on the area rug, and sang "Silent Night." Jenny sat on the rug between Quincy's legs and he had his arms around her. She'd never been happier. She rested against him, loving that there was no more tension in the family.

"I love you," he whispered into her neck.

With those three words, she felt as if she'd won the lottery, and she didn't even need numbers. All she needed was Quincy. Forever.

Epilogue

Three months later...

It had been a whirlwind since Christmas, and Quincy couldn't believe that time had passed so quickly. Since Paxton didn't have a problem with their relationship, they'd gotten married in January in the little Catholic church in Horseshoe with family and friends present. His mother had thrown them a reception at the ranch and then they had taken a ten-day honeymoon to Italy.

Jenny's grandmother, who was Italian, had talked about Italy and Jenny had wanted to see it and maybe look up some distant relatives. They hadn't looked up a soul. They'd been too busy enjoying each other and the beautiful country. He'd promised her they would go back again one day and he intended to keep that promise.

Their living arrangements were a big problem, but they were working it out. He'd offered to buy the trailer that Egan and Rachel lived in while their home was being built. Egan had told him to take it and use it as long as he needed. Quincy had put it by his barn and hooked it up to water and electricity. They had a private place all their own.

Jenny didn't want to be too far away from her dad, and Quincy couldn't be too far away from Grandpa because Grandpa depended on him. Every night at eight they met at the trailer where they spent the night. In the morning Jenny would rush to check on her dad before going to work and he would head for Grandpa's. But they were getting help from Lindsay and Elias. Quincy was proud of the way Elias had stepped up to help so they could have time alone. They were taking it one day at a time, and they both knew they couldn't continue to go from house to house. So Quincy had started building their own home. They'd already poured the slab and Quincy and his brothers would start framing it soon.

They had picked a spot in front of the barn where huge live oak trees, over a hundred years old, grew. Quincy walked around the slab to make sure there were no cracks, and Falcon rode up.

"Looks good," his brother said.

"Yeah, there's a lot of work ahead."

"We'll all be there to help."

"Thanks."

"I just wanted to tell you not to worry about Grandpa tonight. I invited him to eat with us.

He loves playing with the baby. We'll do that more often to give you a break."

"That's really nice of you and Leah."

"We're Rebels and we stand together. Just like you were there for me when Leah was sick. Talk to you later, and don't forget John's first birthday party."

"As if we could forget."

His brother nodded and rode off. Before Quincy could move, Elias came charging in on his horse and dismounted. "This is going to be a big house."

"We're making room for Grandpa and Clyde."

"You don't have to worry about Grandpa. I got your back there. Of course, I don't do anything like you, but he won't starve to death and when I go out, I'll let you know."

Quincy slapped his brother on the back. "I'm real proud of you."

"Now, don't get mushy. When a man gets married, he should be able to live with his wife."

"And you're a philosopher, too."

Elias went back into the saddle. "Don't worry about tonight. I got it covered."

"Falcon said Grandpa was eating with them."

"Hot damn, then I'm going to Rowdy's."

And just like that the old Elias was back. But there was maturity lurking just below the surface.

Quincy pulled out his phone to look at the time. Jenny should be there any minute. She got off work at six and then she would check on her dad and come over. He didn't know how he'd existed before she was in his life. Every day he waited for this moment when she would be all his for the night.

Two arms slipped around his waist from behind and he swung around to gather her closer. After a long kiss, he murmured, "You're early today."

"I sneaked out. Don't tell Lindsay." She laughed that infectious laugh. "Dad's wearing his medical alert bracelet. Can you believe that? He said for me to go be with my husband and that he can take care of himself. He's getting bossy like Lindsay. And speaking of my dear sister, she's at home, so we have the whole night to ourselves. Can you imagine? What will we do?"

He ran his hands through her long hair. "We'll think of something."

She laughed again and he just held her, hardly believing all his dreams had come true.

Someone cleared her throat and they drew apart to see his mother standing there. "I don't mean to interrupt, but I came to see what's been done on the house."

"Just the slab, Mom."

"Your brothers will help you finish it."

"Yeah. We'll probably start next week or when we can work it in."

"I just wanted to tell you I'll fix a plate for Abe and Jude will take it to him, so don't worry about your grandpa."

"Thanks, Mom, but Grandpa is eating at Falcon's tonight." Quincy smiled at his family's efforts to help him, but as Falcon had said, they always stood together.

"Then, I'll do it tomorrow."

"Okay." He wanted to say that he could handle taking care of Grandpa, but his time with Jenny was too valuable. Grandpa needed to get used to other people helping him. But Quincy would never bail on his grandfather.

"This is a perfect spot for a house," his mother was saying.

"Isn't it?" Jenny replied. "We're going to have a long back porch with two rockers so we can sit out here and watch the horses and—" she reached up to kiss Quincy's cheek "—grow old together."

"Oh, dear, you have a long time before that happens." His mother hugged them. "I'm so happy for both of you, and if you need any help with Abe or anything you just let me know."

"Thanks, Mom."

After his mom left, he took Jenny in his arms. "What's the plan?"

"First, we check on White Dove." The horse was due at the end of April and they were watching her closely.

"Then us, that's the plan. Together. Naked. All night long."

He wrapped an arm around her waist and they strolled toward the barn. Dusk was sneaking in and the March wind blew with a noticeable chill, but Quincy was warm and happy. As they walked, he glanced through the darkness, searching for the light that had brought them together. It wasn't there, but he knew when things got rough it would be. He'd never been one to believe in the supernatural, but he believed in love, and he'd found it with a little help from the unknown.

That worked for him.

* * * * *

MILLS & BOON®

Why shop at millsandboon.co.uk?

Each year, thousands of romance readers find their perfect read at millsandboon.co.uk. That's because we're passionate about bringing you the very best romantic fiction. Here are some of the advantages of shopping at www.millsandboon.co.uk:

* **Get new books first**—you'll be able to buy your favourite books one month before they hit the shops

* **Get exclusive discounts**—you'll also be able to buy our specially created monthly collections, with up to 50% off the RRP

* **Find your favourite authors**—latest news, interviews and new releases for all your favourite authors and series on our website, plus ideas for what to try next

* **Join in**—once you've bought your favourite books, don't forget to register with us to rate, review and join in the discussions

Visit **www.millsandboon.co.uk**
for all this and more today!

MILLS_WEB_LP